There were things that needed to be said.

She gathered her courage. "I'm not sure there's much to be gained from going over old ground, but—" she took a breath "—but if I hurt you, I'm sorry."

He stared at the coffee in his cup. "If you hurt me?" he repeated softly. "If?"

He wasn't going to let this be easy. She understood. She deserved this. "When," she corrected. "When I hurt you."

He looked up. "I guess I'd really just like to know what happened."

"You left," she said.

"I enlisted. We had discussed it. You said you would wait."

She had intended to. And she had wanted to. Then things had happened. But nothing she could tell Bray about. Nothing she could ever tell anyone about.

URGENT PURSUIT

BEVERLY LONG

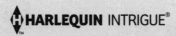

HARLEQUIN INTRIGUE®

To mothers and daughters and the love they share.

Recycling programs
for this product may
not exist in your area.

ISBN-13: 978-0-373-74959-1

Urgent Pursuit

Copyright © 2016 by Beverly R. Long

This edition published by arrangement with Harlequin Books S.A.

For questions and comments about the quality of this book, please contact us at CustomerService@Harlequin.com.

Printed in U.S.A.

www.Harlequin.com

Beverly Long enjoys the opportunity to write her own stories. She has both a bachelor's and a master's degree in business and more than twenty years of experience as a human resources director. She considers her books to be a great success if they compel the reader to stay up way past their bedtime. Beverly loves to hear from readers. Visit beverlylong.com, or like her at Facebook.com/beverlylong.romance.

Books by Beverly Long

Harlequin Intrigue

Return to Ravesville

Hidden Witness
Agent Bride
Urgent Pursuit

The Men from Crow Hollow

Hunted
Stalked
Trapped

The Detectives

Deadly Force
Secure Location

Visit the Author Profile page at Harlequin.com for more titles.

CAST OF CHARACTERS

Summer Wright—She's living a mother's worst nightmare. Her five-year-old daughter, Adie, has been kidnapped. Is she desperate enough to accept help from Brayden Hollister, the man she betrayed fifteen years earlier?

Brayden (Bray) Hollister—The oldest Hollister brother, he's made a life in New York City as a DEA agent. When he's back in Ravesville, he runs into Summer, the woman who had left him almost at the altar. He'd always have done anything for her. That hasn't changed. But can he find her child in time?

Gary Blake—Summer's ex-husband and the father of her two children. He's also an officer on the Ravesville Police Force. What does his sudden disappearance have to do with Adie's kidnapping?

Trish Wright-Roper—As Summer's twin, she knows almost everything about her sister. But even she doesn't know what caused Summer to suddenly marry Gary Blake instead of Bray Hollister.

Charlie Poole—He's the police chief in Ravesville. When Gary Blake disappears, he focuses his investigation on Summer and Bray.

Milo Hernandez—He's a grill cook at the Wright Here, Wright Now Café. Bray is confident that the man is hiding something even though Summer insists that he's a friend.

Flora Wright—Summer's mom is part of a fifteen-year-old secret that has the potential to tear Summer and Bray apart again.

Daniel Stone—This new officer with the Ravesville police department seems to have his own agenda. Is it a mistake for Bray to trust him?

Chapter One

Bray got off the plane in St. Louis, Missouri, and shuffled alongside all the other passengers through the terminal. He'd slept the entire flight, but since it was just over two hours from New York to St. Louis, it was not nearly enough time to make up for the past three months, when any rest in excess of four hours a night was considered a luxury.

And when you made your living working as a drug enforcement agent, *luxury* wasn't part of your everyday vocabulary. But now he had five whole days of downtime, a well-earned vacation as his boss had coined it, to catch up on his sleep.

For months, he'd been planning to travel to Missouri in November for Thanksgiving. Had expected turkey would be served at Chase's upscale, albeit rather sterile, apartment in St. Louis.

Had not imagined Chase would move the event to the family home in Ravesville—or that he'd add something else to the holiday weekend.

He'd been casual, too casual Bray now realized, when he'd asked Bray how he might feel about extending his stay through Sunday. Bray had assumed he was looking for help to get the house ready for sale.

He'd almost fallen off his chair when Chase had announced that he was getting married on the Saturday after Thanksgiving, and would Bray serve as a groomsman? Bray had laughed and said, "Hell, yes." Then Chase, apparently oblivious that at Bray's advanced age of thirty-seven it was good to have some time to adjust to shocks, had kept going. He wanted to buy the family home, to settle in Ravesville with his new wife, Raney.

"Of course," Bray had said. Then added, "Is there anything else?"

All Chase had said was to expect a call from Cal.

He'd had to wait forty-three hours for his youngest brother to call. And when Cal announced that Bray needed to make sure he could get time off for two trips west because he was engaged and would be married at Christmas, Bray hadn't minced words. "I'll come but I'm sure as hell not drinking the water. The Hollister boys are falling fast, and I'm going to save myself."

He was happy for his brothers. But he knew that marriage wasn't for everyone. He'd come close once, but it had been a long time ago. He'd gone to war, and Summer Wright had married somebody else.

Chase had shared that she was divorced with a couple of kids. Still living in Ravesville. Didn't matter. He and Summer were old news.

He stepped up to the car-rental counter and took the keys for the Chevy Impala. In New York, he had a sweet little BMW convertible but he rarely drove it. Paid a hundred bucks a month to park it down the street from his Brooklyn condo. He mostly worked out of an old, beat-up Honda that was owned by the agency. There was nothing on it to steal, and it already had so many dents that the joke was he could run down some scumbag drug dealer and not even have to file a report.

He found his car in the lot and was on the road in less than a minute. Ravesville was ninety miles southwest of St. Louis in the middle of nowhere. He glanced at his watch. With luck, he'd be there for dinner.

There was a lot of traffic for a Tuesday, but finally, when he was twenty minutes out, he called Chase's cell phone.

"Red or white?" he asked when Chase answered.

"We've got plenty of both. Don't worry about

bringing any wine. Meet us at the church on the corner of Main and Portland. You're just in time for rehearsal."

"I could slow way down," Bray said.

"Get your sorry self here. My bride wants to meet you."

At the edge of Ravesville, he saw the gas station where he'd worked his junior and senior years. Like most places, the gas had been self-serve. Bray had worked the inside counter, taking money, selling hot dogs and learning to hate the smell of fountain pop.

Frank Baleeze, who had owned the place, had been his dad's best friend. Once Bray turned sixteen, he'd offered him a job.

It was probably Frank's fault that Bray had become a marine. The man had talked about his years in the corps with such pride. Bray had wanted to be part of something like that.

When Bray had come home for his mother's funeral eight years earlier, Frank had already sold the station and retired to Florida. Even so, Bray stopped in at the old place for gas.

They no longer sold hot dogs, and all the soda was in cans. Their main business was lottery tickets.

It was just more proof that the old saying about not being able to go home again was indeed fact.

The church was close, and Bray found a

place to park. For as long as he could remember, his mother had been a regular attendee at the
Lutheran church. He and his brothers had been
baptized and confirmed here. His parents had both
had their funerals here.

When Bray entered, he saw Chase first, standing next to a very pretty woman with short white-
blond hair. Then there was Cal, with his arm slung
around a stunningly beautiful woman with dark
hair.

Next came hugs and introductions. Once he'd
met Raney and Nalana, he was convinced that
his brothers might have fallen, but they'd landed
in cotton. The women were gorgeous *and* nice.

"Reverend Brown would like us to do a walk-
through," Raney said, pointing to the minister at
the front of the church.

Clara Brown had performed both his father's
and his mother's funerals. She was close to sixty
and had a soft voice, but when she spoke, people
listened. She'd known his mother better, and the
eulogy that she'd delivered had been heartfelt and
poignant, a fitting send-off for a good woman.

Bray waved to her. There was a middle-aged
woman he didn't know sitting at the piano. He
gave her a quick nod and belatedly added a small
smile. His partner on the job would have been
proud. The guy, who'd recently met his one true
love after a nine-month spree of online dating,

was always telling him he needed to do that more. "You're scary tough," Mason would say. "Unapproachable. That turns people away, especially the babes. Try smiling."

Every once in a while, he remembered.

"Nice to see you again, Bray," Reverend Brown said. She stepped off the altar and walked toward them. "Just so you know," she said, looking at Raney, "my ceremonies start and end on time. My assistant will be stationed with you and your attendants in the back of the church. I'm counting on the three of you," she said, switching her gaze to the three Hollister men, "to figure out how to get yourselves out of the back room, through the side door and standing at the altar once the second song starts. Can you manage that?"

"I'll keep him from running out the back door," Bray said.

"No worries there," Chase said, winking at Raney.

"I hope not," Reverend Brown said, a smile in her voice. "It's unfortunate that the maid of honor and other bridesmaid couldn't be here for rehearsal, but I'm counting on the rest of you to fill them in." Bray remembered that Chase had said that Raney wanted her two friends to be able to spend Thanksgiving with their families, so the women wouldn't arrive until late Friday night.

No big deal. How tough could it be to walk down the aisle?

Tough enough that ten minutes later, Reverend Brown was making Raney do it a second *this-time-slower* time when Bray heard the sound of squealing tires and a slamming car door. Seconds later, someone pounding down the church steps to get to the basement. Then shouting. A man, loud. A woman, softer, muffled.

And the hair on the back of his neck stood up.

Raney stopped midaisle, turned and started for the back of the church. Chase caught up with her in just a few steps. Four feet later, Bray clamped a hand on his brother's neck and gently grabbed Raney's arm. "This is your practice," he said. "I've got this."

Both Raney and Chase hesitated, and then Chase gave a quick nod. "Be careful," he said.

When Bray got to the top of the basement stairs, the yelling was still going on. He went fast but quietly down the thirteen steps. Rounded the corner, saw the back of a man and realized that he'd grabbed the person in front of him and was starting to shake them.

"Hey," Bray yelled. And that caused just enough delay that he was able to get across the room, land a hand on the man's shoulder and whip him around.

The man hadn't touched him, but he'd felt as if he'd taken one in the stomach.

He hadn't seen Summer Wright for fifteen years, and there she was. As beautiful as ever with her red hair. Her face was pale, and the fingers she had pressed up to her lips were shaking.

"What the hell?" The man was snarling and pushing at Bray.

Two quick moves and Bray had the man on his knees with his left arm wrenched high behind his back. "Shut up," Bray said calmly.

"Are you okay?" he asked Summer.

She nodded.

So maybe he wouldn't break this man's neck. "What's going on here?" Bray asked.

The man tried to twist away. "I'm having a damn conversation with my wife," he said.

"Ex-wife," Summer said. She swallowed hard and looked at Bray. "You can let him go," she said softly.

So this sorry excuse for a man was Gary Blake. "I don't think so."

She licked her lips. "He'll just make trouble for you if you don't."

Many years ago, Blake had been an officer on the local police force. Based on the uniform, he still was. He leaned close to Blake's ear. "I'm going to let you up," Bray whispered. "But if you make one move in her direction, I'm going to take you down, and I'm going to make it hurt."

When Gary Blake was back on his feet, he whirled toward Bray. "Who the hell are you?" he demanded.

"Bray Hollister."

He could tell the minute the name registered. Blake stood perfectly still, as if debating what to do next. Finally, he turned back toward Summer. "We're not done," he said. Then he walked out of the room.

Bray heard his feet on the stairs, heard the front door, heard a vehicle start. He heard all that while he watched the woman he'd once loved lower herself into a chair, as if her knees were about to give out.

"I figured you'd be home for the wedding," she said.

He didn't answer because he heard more noise on the stairs. Then Chase, Raney, Cal and Nalana were in the basement. Reverend Brown and the piano player were behind them.

"Everything under control?" Chase asked, looking at Bray.

Bray shrugged. Hell, no. He wasn't in control. This woman had broken his heart. She'd chosen someone else. And he'd let that simmer in his gut for years until he'd finally believed he was over her.

And the past five minutes had proved that he'd been lying to himself for years. "Great. Just great."

Raney crossed the room and wrapped an arm around Summer. "Don't worry about these," Raney said. "We'll finish them up."

He'd been so focused on Summer that he'd missed the twenty or so square glass vases that were on the kitchen counter behind her.

Summer shook her head. "Absolutely not," she said, her voice sounding shaky. She cleared her throat. "I've only got a few to wash, and then I'll load them in my van," she added, more confidently.

Raney looked as if she might want to argue, but instead, she gave a quick nod. She looked up at Bray. "I understand you already know Summer."

There wasn't a sound in the room.

"She and her sister, Trish, are handling the flowers and the food for the reception that we're having at the Wright Here, Wright Now Café," Chase finally jumped in. "The church is letting us borrow the vases."

Nobody seemed inclined to want to discuss Gary Blake and what had just happened. Was it because of the potential of Reverend Brown and the other woman hearing the conversation?

Reverend Brown, astute as ever, turned to leave. "Julie and I'll be upstairs. Nice to see you again, Summer."

No one spoke until the door at the top of the stairs opened and closed again.

Then Nalana stepped forward, walking toward the sink where the remaining vases were submerged in soapy water.

Summer held up a hand. "No. Please. I'm almost finished, and I'm sure you all have lots of catching up to do."

The message was clear. *You have to catch up with Bray since he hasn't been around for forever.*

Summer focused on Raney and Chase. "I won't let him ruin any part of your wedding. I promise."

Raney shook her head. "You are not responsible for his poor behavior."

Summer sighed. "I'm just terribly sorry this happened. It's…embarrassing."

"It's not you who should be embarrassed," Chase said. "I think I might have to go drop-kick Blake into the next county."

"Oh, please. I've got a bigger foot and a stronger kick. Let me," Cal said.

That got a small smile from Summer. Bray was happy to see that and happier still to see the easy camaraderie between Chase and Cal. It hadn't always been that way, and he wasn't sure why. But he liked this.

"I'll help Summer finish up here," Bray said.

His brothers exchanged a quick glance. "Well, okay, then," Chase said. He and Cal, each with an arm slung around his woman, went back upstairs, leaving him alone with Summer, who was back on her feet.

"This isn't necessary," she said.

He deliberately rolled up his shirtsleeves, then walked over to the sink and plunged his hands into the lukewarm water. "I'll wash. You dry."

She pressed her lips together. Finally, she let out a loud sigh and grabbed the dull white dish towel.

They didn't talk for the five minutes it took to finish washing the vases. Nor for the seven minutes it took to pack all twenty in two big cardboard boxes. Finally, Bray said, "Now what?"

"Now I load them in my van," she said.

He hoisted a box up. "Lead the way."

She started to lift the other.

"Leave it," he said. "It's too heavy. I'll get it on the second trip."

She led him up the back stairs of the church and outside. There sat an old red van that had seen better days. There were several scratches and a couple of small dents, one that looked pretty new. "What happened here?" he asked, thinking it could have been made by a man's boot. Did Blake take his anger out on objects, too?

She smiled. "Errant football. I said it was a wild throw. Keagan said I should have jumped higher."

"Keagan?"

"My son."

Ahhhh, yes. The child that she'd had with Gary Blake within the first year of their marriage. Bray set the box down, perhaps harder than necessary, but he didn't hear anything break.

He went back inside for the other box. She was standing next to the open van door and stepped aside so that he could shove the box in. Which he did—a little more gently.

"You have a daughter, too, right?" he asked.

Summer's face softened. "Adalyn. We call her Adie. She's five."

"How do they feel about the divorce?" he asked.

There was enough light from the streetlight that he could see her pretty green eyes cloud over. "Probably like any kid feels about a divorce. Sad. Confused. Relieved," she added, her voice quiet.

That pulled at his gut. Was it even possible that Blake had used his fists on them, too? "Did your ex ever—"

She walked to the side of the van, opened the driver's-side door and got in. She started the engine. Finally, she turned her head sideways and made eye contact. "Never. He knew I'd kill him if he did that."

Chapter Two

She had been having a pretty good day until her ex-husband had decided to show up at the church. The restaurant had been pleasantly busy, and when she'd left at two to attend Adie's Thanksgiving Day party at her kindergarten, the sun had been shining and she'd been excited about Chase and Raney's upcoming wedding. She and Trish were determined that the reception was going to be phenomenal. For what Chase was paying them, he deserved something special.

After the party, she'd driven Adie home and waited another half hour for Keagan to get home from school. It was his first year at Ravesville High, and he detested it when she picked him up in the van. "I'm not a little kid," he'd say.

He wasn't. But neither was a fourteen-year-old boy an adult. She was full-time busy trying to balance her natural tendency to keep him close and protected with the reality that she needed to let go, let him have more independence, let him make more decisions, even let him make a few mistakes.

When she'd been that age, she'd been an adult. Out of necessity. What was it Trish used to say? *We were pushed out of the nest early, and we had to either fly or crash.* They'd flapped their wings hard and managed to stay in the air, taking turns buying groceries, cooking dinner, doing laundry.

They'd had each other, and together, they'd managed to mostly hide a big secret.

She didn't want anything like that for Keagan. Generally, all she really hoped for was for him to pick up his clothes off the floor and shower regularly.

Today, once he'd got home, they'd had a brief conversation, which mainly consisted of her brightly telling him about her day and asking about his and getting a few grunts in response. Then she'd left him in charge of Adie. In the past, she'd have had her mom come over to watch the kids. They loved having Grandma at the house. But in the past year or so, if she was going to be gone for only an hour or so at a time, Keagan watched Adie so that he could earn some baby-sitting money to buy a new bike.

She was proud of him for realizing that he needed to work for the money, that she simply wouldn't be able to hand over a couple hundred dollars. The restaurant was doing well, and she and Trish were able to take small salaries, but by the time she paid rent and all the other assorted bills of raising children, there was little left.

She couldn't count on Gary. He was now over six months behind in child support. And he had become more and more volatile over the past months. She still had sore ribs that substantiated that today's incident had not been an isolated event.

But never before had it been a public event, and she was mortified. Bad enough that Chase and Cal Hollister and their wonderful fiancées should witness it, but having Bray be the one to break it up had been almost more than she could be expected to bear.

He looked fabulous. He had his thick brown hair pulled back into a little ponytail at the nape of his neck, and the short beard he wore, which was so popular now, made him look super sexy and…well, even a little dangerous.

And when he'd had Gary on his knees, practically begging for relief, it had been easy to see that it wasn't false advertising. He'd always been a tough guy. Probably why the Marines had been a natural fit. And now that he was a DEA agent, his natural persona had been fine-tuned and he was sleek and dangerous.

Gary wasn't that tough, but he did play dirty, and she'd tried to warn Bray. Bray would find his car towed for parking too close to a fire hydrant or get a ticket for going thirty-four in a thirty-mile-an-hour zone. Or worse. He'd come out after an evening meal and find his windshield cracked or his tires flat. That was what had happened to the one man Summer had dated postdivorce. Needless to say, the poor guy hadn't bothered to call again.

And she was powerless to do anything about Gary. Because he knew the secret. He was part of the secret.

At the intersection, she stopped at the four-way sign. To the left was the Wright Here, Wright Now Café. At night, it was under Trish's careful watch, allowing Summer to be home with the kids. If she went to the café tonight, her twin would instantly sense that something was wrong, and she'd force Summer to blurt out the truth.

No, she'd leave the vases in the van tonight and unload them tomorrow. She wasn't ready to deal with her reaction to Bray, let alone talk about it to someone else. Plus, she'd probably left Keagan and Adie alone together for long enough. She turned right and drove the mile to her house. It wasn't until she was pulling into the one-car attached garage that she noticed the car behind her.

For a quick minute, she thought it might be Gary, back for round two. But it wasn't.

She got out and faced Bray Hollister, who was acting as if he had every right to follow her home and park in her driveway. "What are you doing here?" she said, almost wincing when she heard how bitchy she sounded.

It was just that seeing him again after so many years was too much. She hadn't had time to prepare, time to put up her defenses. She'd been ready for him to be at the wedding reception, and she'd already planned on how she would handle the encounter. She'd be polite, a little distant, too busy to chat for long.

Now she felt naked and raw from her encounter with Gary, and she wasn't sure she had the emotional maturity to go up against the only man she'd ever really loved.

"I wanted to make sure you got home okay."

"Oh." She felt so very small. And mean. "Thank you."

They stared at each other. She could hear Mitzi barking and glanced over Bray's shoulder. Across the street, she could see the small white dog through the window. She was on the back of the couch, her nose pressed to the glass.

Bray turned his head to look.

"That's Trudy Hudder's house," Summer said.

"Junior English?" Bray asked.

She nodded. Mrs. Hudder had introduced literature to every student in Ravesville for forty years before retiring a few years earlier.

Adie liked to play with the dog. Would listen to hear Mitzi outside and then sneak out for a quick couple of dog kisses.

Summer whipped around to make sure her children were not at the door or with their own noses pressed up against the window. The blinds were down, thank goodness. Sometimes Keagan forgot to do that when it got dark. She turned back to Bray.

"It's been a long time," he said. "I thought we might get a drink or something."

"I can't. My children are home alone."

"You have a coffeepot?"

Bray had always loved coffee, from the time he'd been a teenager. Her, too. They'd been the only sixteen-year-olds who ordered coffee with their pizza. She should lie. Tell him she gave it up years ago. When she married someone else.

"I do," she said.

"Works for me." He took a couple of steps toward her, closing the ten-foot gap.

This was such a bad idea. She'd avoided having a conversation with this man for fifteen years. Had been hoping to avoid it for another fifteen. She held up her hand.

He stopped.

Bray would not force his way in. That had never been his way. He had always been a gentleman.

She could give him ten minutes. She owed him much more. She motioned with her hand for him to follow her.

They went into the house through the garage. When they stepped into the kitchen, she could hear the television blaring in the family room. There were dirty dishes on the counter that hadn't been there when she'd left less than two hours ago. There was also a big splotch of milk on the floor, as if Adie might have been trying to pour a glass and the jug had been too heavy.

She just couldn't worry about it now.

"I'm home," she yelled.

"Mama," Adie said. Feet came thundering around the corner.

Summer leaned down and scooped up her little girl. "Hey, slow down," she said, holding her tight.

Adie squirmed in her arms. She pointed to Bray. "Who's that?"

"This is Mr. Hollister," Summer said.

Bray waved. "Hi, Adie. How about you just call me Bray. That's a lot easier to say."

"Bray," Adie repeated. "Like *neigh*," she said, making the sound of a horse.

Bray smiled. "Exactly."

Adie turned back to her. "You're late," she said. "We're hungry."

"I know, sweetheart. I'll start dinner in just a few minutes," she said. She let Adie slide down her body. Once the little girl's feet hit the ground, she was off.

"Mom's home and there's a man with her." Adie's voice floated back to them.

The volume on the television went down. In came Keagan, his thin shoulders slouched forward, his too-long hair in his eyes.

She reached out a hand to ruffle his hair. He jerked away. He was staring at Bray.

"Thanks for watching Adie," Summer said. "This is Bray Hollister. We...we were in school together."

Bray stepped forward, extended his hand. It took Keagan a second, but he stuck his arm out.

"Nice to meet you, Keagan. I understand you like football."

Keagan didn't answer. He turned to his mother. "I thought you were going to the church for vases."

"I...did. Remember, it's Chase Hollister who is getting married. Well, Bray is Chase's older brother. He's home for the wedding."

"Dad stopped by," Keagan said.

"When?" she asked quickly.

"Right after you left."

Thank goodness. She'd hoped he hadn't come by after the incident at the church. "I saw him. He stopped by the church."

"He seemed upset about something."

He had seemed more volatile than usual. A simple conversation about switching the weekend the kids would be at his house had gone south so fast that she still wasn't sure what had set him off. He hadn't looked good, either. There had been dark circles under his pale blue eyes, as if he hadn't slept well for some time.

Maybe trouble at work. Gossip had been swirling recently about a fight between Gary and a newly hired officer named Daniel Stone. Nobody seemed to have the details, and neither Gary nor Daniel was talking about it. Probably at the direction of Chief Poole. He was probably embarrassed that his small department was a topic of conversation.

But she'd officially given up making excuses for Gary's behavior when she'd signed the divorce paperwork. Never ran him down in front of the kids, but didn't try to build him up to be father of the year, either. "You don't need to worry about your dad," she said. "Did you do your homework?"

He gave her the *you're so stupid* look. "We don't have school until next Monday."

That was right. Tomorrow was the day before Thanksgiving, and the kids were getting a nice long holiday. "Well, you can watch a little more television. Just keep the volume down," she suggested.

Keagan looked between her and Bray. "What are you going to be doing?"

The bad mother in her so wanted to tell him that it was none of his business. Since starting high school three months earlier, Keagan had got progressively more distant, rarely volunteering any conversation and definitely not interested in anything Summer was doing.

But she was the adult. Supposedly smarter, more mature. "I'm going to have a little conversation with Mr. Hollister and then I'm going to fix dinner. I'll call you when it's ready," she said.

He took the hint and shuffled out of the kitchen. The small space got quiet again. She got busy making a small pot of coffee. Out of the corner of her eye, she saw Bray grab a paper towel off the roll and wipe up the spilled milk on the floor. He found the garbage under her sink.

"Thanks," she said. She scooted around the dirty dishes on the counter. She still missed having a dishwasher, but the house had been perfect in so many other ways for the three of them that she hadn't quibbled over small things. It was in a safe neighborhood and she could afford it. Those were the important things.

When the coffee was done, she poured cups for both her and Bray and carried them over to the kitchen table, where Bray had taken a seat. "Cream or sugar?" she asked.

"Black. Like always," he said.

Some things never changed, but some things had changed so much there was no going back. She took a sip too soon and burned her tongue. Still, for lack of anything better to do, she took another one. Finally, she set her cup down. "So, how was your flight?" she asked.

He took a sip of his own coffee. "It's been a long time, Summer. You really want to talk about my travel?"

Hell, no. But everything else was fraught with danger. One wrong step and it could blow up. But yet there were things that needed to be said. She gathered her courage. "I'm not sure there's much to be gained from going over old ground, but..." She took a breath. "But if I hurt you, I'm sorry."

He stared at the coffee in his cup. "If you hurt me?" he repeated softly. "If?"

He wasn't going to let this be easy. She understood. She deserved this. "When," she corrected. "When I hurt you."

He looked up. "I guess I'd really just like to know what happened."

"You left," she said.

"I enlisted. We had discussed it. You said you would wait."

She had intended to. And she had wanted to. Then things had happened. But nothing she could tell Bray about. Nothing she could ever tell anyone about. "I met someone," she said. It was the story she'd stuck to for fifteen years.

"Gary Blake."

She nodded.

"He's a real prize," Bray said, his tone bitter.

Gary hadn't always been this way. In the beginning, he'd been…fine. Attentive. Hardworking. And she'd thought it would be enough. "Bray, did you ever marry?" she asked tentatively.

"Nope."

The silence in the room stretched out. Finally, Bray shifted in his chair. "At the church, you said that Gary had never beaten your kids. There was something you didn't say."

"What's that?"

"That he'd never beaten you."

She was so weary. So damn tired of protecting everybody else's interests. "He didn't. And I would not have thought him capable of it. But about two months ago, we got into an argument because he was supposed to pay some fees for Keagan's sports. But he was really late and the coach had told me that he was going to have to suspend Keagan. Gary got really mad and pushed me down. And…and then he kicked me. My back got pretty bruised up."

She saw a wave of emotion cross his handsome face. "Kicked you like a stray dog," he said, his tone bitingly sharp.

She put her hand out. Touched him. His skin was so warm. "It's over," she said.

"Did you report it to the police?"

"He is the police."

"He's got to have a boss."

She shrugged. "I made a decision. I did what was best for me and my family."

"By what happened today, I don't think he's turned over a new leaf. The next time he might really hurt you. What are you going to tell your children when you've got a broken jaw and a busted eye socket?"

The image made her sick. "That's not going to happen," she said.

"Maybe somebody needs to make sure of that," he said.

She stood up. "Don't you even think about getting involved, Bray Hollister. You can't waltz back in here and...and mess things up."

"Mess things up? Honey, I thought that was your department."

She would not cry. She would not. "My children are hungry," she said, her voice flat. "If you'll excuse me, I'm going to fix them dinner." She walked over to the door that led to the garage, opened it and reached to turn on the garage light.

She heard a sharp bark and saw that Mitzi was outside, peeing in the front yard. Trudy, already in her nightgown, stood on the front porch, staring across the street. Great.

Bray followed her out of the house. She stood to the side and let him walk past.

Trudy waved. "Nice to see you again, Brayden. I wondered if you'd be back for the wedding."

"Wouldn't miss it," Bray said. "Nice to see you again, Mrs. Hudder."

She wondered how he could sound so polite. Her voice would have come out strangled. She felt as if her throat were closing up.

Without a backward glance, Bray got in his car and started it. He backed out of the driveway and sedately drove off.

Fifteen years ago, there'd been screaming tires and a racing engine.

She closed the garage door, went back inside her house and then very carefully let herself slide down the back of the door until she was sitting on the floor.

Then she started to cry.

Bray texted Cal, telling him that he wouldn't be there for dinner. It was the chicken's way out, he knew, but he simply wasn't up to the questions that either would be asked or, if everyone decided to give him a pass, would be hanging in the air, hovering, threatening to smother them all.

So, what was it like, seeing Summer after all these years?

Jarring. Exhilarating. Disappointing. Painful. His emotions were all over the place.

She was still beautiful. He'd always loved her red hair. In high school, she'd worn it longer, but now it just touched her shoulders. Her skin was still lovely, freckle-free unlike most redheads. There were a few lines by her pale green eyes that hadn't been there fifteen years ago, but still, she looked more like twenty-seven than thirty-seven.

Her children were the undisputable proof that the years had truly gone by. Adie was a doll, with her strawberry blonde hair and her big blue eyes. And Keagan, well, he supposed he'd be a good-looking kid if he bothered to get rid of the disdain that poured off his skinny adolescent frame.

Bray appreciated that the kid had hoofed it into the kitchen quickly upon hearing that his mother had brought home a man. That told him something. It didn't happen often. Not that that mattered. Summer hadn't said it, but the message had been clear. *We're done. Been done for a long time.*

When he'd first heard that Chase and Raney intended to get married in Ravesville, he'd fleetingly wondered if he might run into Summer while he was home. He hadn't dwelled on the possibility, had merely considered it, decided that it would be no big deal and moved on.

All that proved was that at age thirty-seven, he was living in denial, maybe not all that different from a kid hooked on meth who said he could stop anytime he wanted.

He drove through Ravesville, making a full stop at the end of every block. The same irritating four-way stop signs had been there when he'd been seventeen. Then, he'd done a casual rolling stop, too cool in his old Cutlass convertible to be bothered by rules. And more often than not, Summer had been at his side, her pretty red hair blowing in the wind.

He turned right at the edge of town. Just like old times. On most warm nights, of which there were a lot in Missouri, he and Summer had gone to Rock Pond, the local swimming hole.

They never did a whole lot of swimming there. Instead, he'd pull the old sheet out of his trunk, spread it on the ground, and in the dark of night, he'd make love to Summer.

And afterward, she would cling to him, her sweet young body so firm, yet so soft, and tell him that she loved him and that she would always be his.

As he drove onto the property, he could see that they were still actively working parts of the old quarry, still blasting away. He went around the bend in the narrow road, got close to the section that had been filled with water for many years and killed his lights. It was not a warm night. Not much chance of encountering naked teens doing grown-up things. With little care for the cold, he got out of the car, boosted himself up onto the hood and leaned back against the windshield. He put his hands behind his head and stared up at the sky.

He'd been a half a world away, trying not to get blown up, and the memories of this place, his time with Summer here, had kept him sane.

Everything happened for a reason. That was the mantra that his mother had lived by. Even when her husband had died too young, leaving her with three adolescent boys to raise, she'd said those words. Even when she married Brick Doogan, who hadn't an ounce of the character that his dad had.

He'd survived four years in the military when others hadn't. He'd clawed his way back after learning that the girl he'd left behind had married someone else, and he eventually got a college degree on Uncle Sam's dime and a job in New York. Others had come back too screwed up to do the same. He managed to keep a whole lot of drugs off the streets and a bunch of unknown kids alive without getting a knife in his gut when others bought it. He'd built a very satisfactory life and pushed the old memories to the back of the virtual closet, where they belonged.

But now they were clawing to get out, ripping apart his gut, making him want to howl at the quarter moon.

He slid off the hood, got in and turned his car around. When he got to the end of the long lane, he turned right instead of left. He still wasn't quite ready to go home. He drove through town. At the edge, he turned around. Drove down the main street again. Killing time.

Not true. He was looking for Gary Blake. He might as well admit the truth.

Somebody needed to teach him a lesson, and right now, it would feel damn good to put his fist through something. It might as well be Blake's face.

He pulled over and used his smartphone to find Blake's address. He recognized the street. As he drove the six blocks, he knew he was probably about to do something really stupid.

But sometimes a man just had to do what he needed to do.

Chapter Three

Bray was nursing his third cup of coffee when he heard the sound of a car pulling into the Hollister driveway. Chase and Cal were at the sink, washing and drying, because Raney and Nalana had cooked breakfast. He, as the honored guest, was getting to sit.

Which was helpful since he was fighting a headache that was likely a combination of jet lag, long-term fatigue and one too many beers. He'd come home around midnight. The house had been dark, but it had been easy enough to find his way upstairs, avoiding the step that squeaked and finally getting into the brand-new bed that was the centerpiece of his newly decorated bedroom.

Raney and Chase were making a home of the old place. It was unexpected, sort of like the new camaraderie between Chase and Cal. He was going to ask about that. Sometime. Just not now, when the brain cells weren't yet all firing.

He heard the sound of a door opening and shutting. "Expecting someone?" he asked.

Chase looked at Raney and she shook her head. Cal walked down the hallway to look out the front door.

"It's Poole," he said.

"Who's Poole?" Bray asked.

Cal walked back into the kitchen, exchanged a quick look with Chase and said, "The police chief. Anything we need to know about last night?"

Bray shook his head. "Why look at me?"

Nalana smiled. "Because the rest of us were in bed by nine o'clock."

Bray returned the smile. "That's because my brothers are both lucky sons of…guns." He pushed back his chair. "I might as well get this."

He waited for the knock. Counted to five, then opened the door. On the other side was a man, probably midsixties, his belly hanging over his belt, looking as if a fast walk, let alone a real chase after an enemy, would take him down.

"Bray Hollister?" the man asked.

"Yes."

"I'm police chief Poole. I'd like to ask you a few questions."

He heard a rustle in the kitchen and knew that if he gave any indication that he was uncomfortable with the request, his brothers were going to figure out a way to get Poole off their porch.

"Sure," he said. "Come on in."

He led the chief into the living room and motioned for him to have a seat. The man sat in the armchair, making the cushions sink. Bray sat on the couch and relaxed back against a pillow.

"I understand you arrived in town yesterday."

"That's correct."

"From New York." The man practically wrinkled his nose.

Bray nodded. He was tempted to make a joke that living in the city wasn't a crime the last time he'd checked. But he kept his mouth shut. Poole was uncomfortable, and that was making Bray doubly so.

"And you drove straight to Ravesville from the St. Louis airport?"

"Yes."

"And what did you do once you got to town?"

"I went to the church on the corner of Main and Portland. My brother is getting married there this weekend."

"And you had some conversation with Gary Blake?"

"Conversation? Is that what he called it?" Bray asked. He was disgusted. The guy tried to rough up his ex-wife and then whined to his boss because Bray had got the better of him.

"I didn't speak with Gary. Julie Wentworth is my sister-in-law. She plays the piano every Sunday and for almost every wedding in town."

Piano player Julie and Reverend Brown had not witnessed his physical interaction with Blake. They would only be able to report on what they'd overheard.

Not true. They would be able to support that Summer had been upset—to the point that her voice had been shaking.

"I understand you and Summer Wright were an item in high school. That was before my time in Ravesville. Is that correct?"

An item? "We dated," he said. If Poole wanted to know more than that, he was going to have to ask somebody else.

"Uh-huh. So, after you left the church, where did you go?" Poole asked.

Bray made sure his face showed no reaction. But his brain, which might have been idle in the kitchen, was now working itself back to fighting weight. "I went to Summer's house."

"Why?"

"She had some vases in the back of her van. They were heavy. I thought she might need some help carrying them."

"How long were you there?"

Bray sat up, feeling as if his pancakes were

going to be on the chief's shoes. "Did something happen to Summer? To one of the kids?"

He was going to kill Gary Blake.

The chief shook his head. "I drove by the Wright Here, Wright Now Café on my way here. I verified that Summer was working her shift, as usual. Therefore, I assume her children are fine."

Verified. The man had made sure Summer was working. So whatever was wrong, Summer and her family were involved in some way.

"If there's nothing else," Bray said, standing up. He had things to do.

Poole didn't take the hint. "What time did you leave Summer's house and where did you go?"

Bray had a fairly good idea the man already knew what time he'd left. Perhaps he'd talked to Mrs. Hudder. He decided to cut to the chase. "I left around seven. Drove around town for a while." No need to tell him that he'd driven to Blake's house, that he'd pounded on the door, wanting the son of a bitch to have the guts to show his face. "I was hungry, so I went to the One Toe In Bar and Grill for a cheeseburger and some beers."

"What time did you leave the bar?"

"Close to midnight. Why?"

"Anybody there going to be able to verify that?"

He'd sat alone in a back booth, but he'd had the same waitress for most of the evening. He assumed she'd be able to. "I think so."

"You better hope so, Mr. Hollister."

Bray shrugged. "Look, I've been a good sport and answered all your questions. Now why don't you tell me why the hell you're asking them?" Maybe Gary Blake's pride had been more damaged than he'd thought and the man had gone to his boss to complain about his interaction with Bray. If he had, that was pretty damn stupid. Nothing like hanging out your own dirty laundry.

Chief Poole hefted himself out of the chair. He pulled up his pants and they immediately sagged below his belly again. "Gary Blake was scheduled to start work at seven this morning. When he didn't show, Officer Stone drove to his house."

"And?" Bray prompted when the police chief stopped.

"And Gary wasn't there."

"Big deal," Bray said. "Maybe he got his days mixed up and he thought he had a vacation day. He's out shopping for a turkey right now."

"There were signs of a very fast exit from the house. A small amount of blood at the scene."

He could see Summer's eyes, hear the sincerity in her voice. *He knew I'd kill him if he did that.* "So, he cut himself shaving and went to the emergency room."

"Maybe," Chief Poole said. "But, you know, police officers make a lot of enemies."

Bray wanted to see Blake's house. Cops in small

towns weren't well trained in investigating crime scenes—they simply didn't see enough of them.

But as much as he wanted to view the scene, he wanted to see Summer more. He had to know what she'd done. Had his questions about Blake spurred on memories that she'd been unable to deal with?

"How long are you expecting to be in town, Mr. Hollister?"

"Through Sunday."

"And you're staying here at this house?"

Bray nodded.

"Good," the chief said. "I want to know where I can find you if I have more questions."

Bray didn't answer. He simply watched the man walk to the front door and let himself out. He counted to three before his brothers got to the living room.

They each had the same worried look in their eyes. Probably right now were thinking of good defense attorneys.

"Listen," he said, "I didn't do anything to Gary Blake."

"Blood at the scene," Chase said.

"Small amount. I heard the man," Bray said, irritated. He'd been back in town for less than a day, and Gary Blake, who had caused him so much heartache years ago when he'd married Bray's girl, was still causing trouble. "There's probably a list of people a page long that want to get Blake for one reason or another."

"Summer," Cal said.

Bray didn't say anything.

"You don't think she did something, do you?" Chase asked.

Bray had no idea what Summer was capable of. "I don't know," he said. "But I think I better ask her."

SUMMER HAD REALLY never thought much about Charlie Poole. He'd been Gary's boss for about five years. He was polite to her when he came into the restaurant, ordered two eggs and bacon with a side of biscuits and gravy every day of his life, and tipped poorly.

She'd never had cause to worry about him until now, when he'd come in and asked if he could speak to her privately.

"We don't have much private space," she said.

He said nothing. She put down her coffeepot, led him back to the kitchen, smiled at Milo, the grill cook, to let him know that everything was okay and took a spot in the corner, where she could keep an eye on the dining room through the small window in the swinging door.

She felt sick when the chief told her why he was there. Gary. Missing. Blood at the scene. An open gallon of milk on the table. A half-eaten bowl of cereal. The back door unlocked and not closed tight.

What the hell? Her first thoughts were of her children. What would she tell them?

But before she could get her head around it, Chief Poole started asking questions.

"I understand you were at the church yesterday," he said. "That you and Gary were in the basement."

Julie had probably mentioned it to her brother-in-law. She was a lovely piano player but a terrible gossip.

"Yes."

"I didn't think you two had much to do with each other anymore."

"We share children," she said. "This coming weekend was Gary's weekend to have them, but he needed to switch."

"Why?"

She'd wondered the same thing. Normally, it wouldn't have been a big deal to switch. But because she would be busy catering the wedding, she'd pushed back a little. That had seemed to set him off. "I don't know."

"So after you left the church, you went straight home?"

"Yes." It dawned on her that the chief hadn't asked any questions about what had happened at the church between her and Gary. Was it because

Julie had given him enough that he'd realized that his second-in-command might have been in the wrong and he didn't want any additional documentation of the fact?

And speaking of documentation, the chief wasn't making any notes. He had yet to pull his notebook from his pocket. In his left breast pocket, he had the same kind of notebook that Gary never went anywhere without. Once, early on in the marriage, she hadn't realized that he hadn't removed it from his pocket and she'd put it in the washing machine. That had caused a crisis that involved attempting to dry out thirty or so small pages because he'd needed those quick notations to fill out the endless reports that he'd hated.

Maybe the chief had a really good memory. Or maybe he realized that she didn't have anything to gain by harming Gary.

"And did you have any visitors last night?" he asked.

She wasn't trained in police work, but thought she might be a better interrogator than the chief. He clearly already knew that she had indeed had a visitor. Perhaps he'd already spoken to Mrs. Hudder. Or to Bray.

He'd been upset when he'd left her house. She'd known that he was having difficulty dealing with what she'd told him. Had he taken out his anger on Gary?

Had Bray become sucked into the tangled relationship that she had with her ex? It was a horrifying thought. When would her bad decisions stop hurting Bray Hollister?

She was confident that he would tell the truth, that he would not run from it. He'd always had more character than her. "Bray Hollister stopped by. He didn't stay long. Then I fixed my children dinner, watched some television and went to bed by ten."

"Can anyone verify that you were home all evening?" he asked.

Had she been wrong about his intent? Was she really a…suspect? She pressed her hand to her empty stomach.

Hell, yes, there were times I wanted him gone, she wanted to say. But admitting that she'd spent valuable time she didn't have as a single parent imagining how nice it would be if he would simply disappear wasn't going to help her.

"No," she said. "But I was." She looked through the small window in the door and saw that four new customers had come in while she'd been talking with the chief. They were looking around, staring wistfully at the coffeepot, probably wondering where the heck she was. "I really need to get back to the dining room," she said. As Milo flipped his pancakes, he was slapping the flat end of his stainless-steel spatula on the hot grill, letting her know that he was watching and ready to assist if she needed it.

"Just a couple more questions," Chief Poole said, holding up his hand. "Has Gary ever done this before, just disappear unexpectedly?"

Once or twice toward the end of their marriage, he'd been gone for a few days. *Getting his head together.* That was what he always told her. She suspected that involved a stack of chips and a deck of cards, but by then, she hadn't really cared enough to probe.

"Sometimes to fish or to gamble." It dawned on her that the chief probably knew Gary as well as she did. That made this an even more awkward conversation.

The chief nodded. "I probably should check to see if his rods are still there."

She didn't say anything, hoping he'd get the hint and leave.

"Do you know anybody who had a particular beef with Gary?"

She sighed. "He's been a cop in the same community for more than fifteen years. I imagine there are any number of people who aren't fond of him. The speed trap out by the high school is particularly irritating and probably hasn't endeared him to many."

"Anybody with a complaint more serious than a moving violation?"

"You'd know better about that than me," she said.

"I may want to talk to your children."

"Not without me, and not until I've talked to them first," she said, her voice stern. She didn't care if he was the police chief.

"I'll be in touch," he said. He took a step. Stopped. "I'd appreciate it if you'd keep this conversation between us," he said. "You know how gossip spreads in Ravesville."

She did. And it would make people uneasy if they thought that something had happened to one of their police officers.

She nodded, and Chief Poole pushed open the swinging door, walked the length of the café and left through the front entrance. Thirty seconds later, Summer followed him out of the kitchen, smiling, greeting customers, putting on the show of her life. But her head was whirling. So much so that she delivered eggs instead of French toast to one of her favorite customers. Apologizing profusely, she ran back to the kitchen to get the order replaced.

"What's going on?" Milo asked.

"I'll tell you later," Summer promised.

She took another quick minute to pull her cell phone from her pocket. She pressed the button for

Gary's number. It went straight to voice mail. She waited for the beep. "Gary, it's Summer. Listen, please call me. It's important." She pressed End.

Maybe she should call Trish, too. She knew Gary pretty well. Maybe she would have some ideas.

No. It wasn't the type of news a person delivered over the phone.

Was the chief serious that he intended to talk to her kids? Would he wait and give Gary time to show himself?

For the first time in a very long time, she wished she could suddenly make Gary appear. What the hell was he up to now? Was it possible that he was really in trouble? Did this have anything to do with the absolutely horrible mood he'd been in?

She had lots of questions and no answers. She went back to the dining area and cleared two dirty tables.

She heard the soft tinkle of a bell and looked to the front door. Bray Hollister, his expression giving nothing away, walked in and took a seat at the counter. He wore blue jeans, a blue-and-gray flannel shirt, a dark gray insulated vest and cowboy boots. Every woman's eyes in the place followed him, whether they were twenty years old or sixty. He positively oozed sex appeal.

She contemplated going back to the kitchen for

the rest of her life. "Morning," she said, mindful that just three stools away were other customers. "Coffee?" she asked, holding up the pot.

Bray nodded.

She poured the cup and slid it in his direction. He took a sip. "Busy day?" he asked.

"Busy enough," she said.

"Had a visit from the chief yet?" His voice was pitched low.

"Yeah. You?"

He nodded. "Are you doing okay?" he asked.

No. She was a mess. "I think so."

"Got anything you need to tell me?" he asked.

"I was about to ask you the same thing."

He shook his head. "I didn't touch your ex."

She believed him. Relief flooded her system. "I didn't, either."

He studied her. Then nodded. "Okay, then. What now?"

"Now I figure out what the hell happened to Gary before it bleeds over and affects me or our children."

Chapter Four

"But before I do that," she said, "I have to talk to my kids. Chief Poole said he might need to question them."

Bray picked up a sugar packet. Set it down. "He's doing his job. A man is missing. A cop. He needs to turn over every rock that he can."

"But they're my rocks. My baby rocks," she said.

She would be the kind of mother who would protect her children with her last breath. "They might know something and not even realize it. You might, too," he said, his tone suggestive. "Tell me about your ex."

"I've got customers to wait on," she said, clearly not interested in his suggestion. He understood. He really didn't want to talk about the son of a bitch, either. There weren't many that could make the claim, but Gary Blake had bested Bray, in all the ways it counted. Reason enough to hate him.

If Blake was screwing around somewhere, oblivious to the concern he'd left behind, dismissive of the blow his children would bear when they heard he was missing, well, Bray was going to hand him his lunch, and the guy would need a blender and a straw to eat it. "What time does Trish come in to relieve you?"

"Normally at two and works until nine. But it's Thanksgiving eve, so we're not open tonight. The café will close at two today and reopen at six on Friday morning. And with any luck, Gary will come in for his coffee to go at eight thirty, just like every other day."

"You're still going to talk to your kids today?"

She nodded. "I have to pick them up at Trish's. She's babysitting. I know I need to do this but I'm not sure what to tell them."

"The truth. But maybe not the whole truth."

She let out a huff. "That's my specialty," she said in a disgusted tone. Then she walked away.

What the hell did she mean by that? Bray contemplated that question for the next three hours as he sat on the stool. Summer stopped filling his coffee cup and generally ignored him until he flagged her down and ordered a grilled ham-and-cheese sandwich for lunch. She hadn't said a word when she'd slid the plate in his direction, but it didn't escape his notice that she'd remembered to add a side of mayonnaise so that he could dip his French fries.

Finally, ten minutes after she'd put the closed sign in the window, all the other customers were gone except him. "I'm going with you when you talk to your children," he said.

"They don't know you."

"I'm not going for them. I'm going for you."

That shut her up. She got out the vacuum and plugged it in. He grabbed it out of her hand. "Let me help," he said. "You can get out of here faster."

It had been driving him crazy for the past three hours watching her literally fly around the room. Taking orders, clearing tables, making pot after pot of coffee, taking cash at the register up front. He'd wanted to jump in and help but had known that would spread like wildfire through the small town. The fact that he'd been sitting at the counter for an extended period probably already had tongues wagging. He'd recognized a few people from his high school days. Had nodded at one or two, but nobody had approached to engage in conversation.

After the floor had been vacuumed and the counters wiped down, and she'd rolled a tray of clean silverware into white napkins, Summer excused herself to use the restroom. Seconds later, the cook pushed through the swinging door.

"Who are you?" he asked, his voice flat.

"Bray Hollister." He'd been gone a long time, but he was pretty good with faces. He didn't think he'd ever met this man. He was probably midfifties, slight build but wiry, with hair pulled back into a ponytail like Bray. However, his was much longer and almost black. His face had several scars, none of which he'd got from working behind a grill. "Who are you?" Bray asked.

"That's not important. What's important is that you understand that Summer and Trish Wright are special to me. If you mess with them, you mess with me. And that would be a mistake on your part."

Most people wouldn't even attempt to intimidate Bray. But this guy was a natural. Bray appreciated his intensity and willingness to take him on.

He was glad that this man was in Summer's corner. "I don't intend to mess with either of them. I'm an old friend." Bray heard the bathroom door open.

"I'll be watching you," Milo said.

"All finished?" Summer asked the cook.

"Thirty minutes. Then I'm out of here."

"Don't work too late," she said. "Uh, Milo, this is Bray Hollister. He used to live in Ravesville. Bray, Milo Hernandez. Best grill cook this side of the Mississippi."

If she noticed the stillness between the two men, she ignored it. "Milo, I have something to tell you."

The cook looked at Bray.

"He can stay," Summer said. "He knows."

And in a very controlled way, Summer told the man about her conversation with Chief Poole, the suspicions that foul play might be involved. His expression never changed.

"The chief asked me to keep this quiet, but I wanted you to know," she said. "You're like family."

"What can I do to help?" he asked.

She shook her head. "Keep your ears open. If you hear anything, call me right away." She gave the man a quick hug. Over her shoulder, he made eye contact with Bray.

"I've got this," Bray mouthed.

The man gave a sharp nod. "Call me if you need me, Summer." He went back into the kitchen.

"He's something," Bray said.

"He was a godsend," she said quietly. "He arrived in Ravesville just weeks after Rafe's death." She looked at him. "You may not know. Trish was married. To Rafe Roper. He wasn't from around here. But he worked construction, and when they built the new mall near Hamerton, he rented a house near here. Trish fell hard and fast, and they got married just months after he arrived in town.

But sadly, just nine months later, he went on a float trip, you know the kind, with inner tubes and coolers of beer. Somehow he got separated from his buddies and drowned."

"Poor Trish." He had always really liked Summer's twin.

"It was horrible. The worst of it all was that his body was never recovered. Trish was devastated. She couldn't work. I couldn't expect her to. I thought we would lose the restaurant for sure. I couldn't keep it going on my own. And then Milo turned up."

"Out of the blue?"

"He'd been in prison. Not a lot of places will give an ex-con a job."

"But you did."

"From the very beginning it felt right. He saved us. Worked like a dog. And then when Trish finally was able to come back, he stayed."

"I think he's fond of the two of you."

"It's mutual. He didn't like Gary. I think it was the natural dislike between a cop and an ex-con."

Maybe. Or maybe Milo was just a good judge of character. But he didn't say that. There was nothing to be gained from running down Blake at this point.

Summer shut most of the lights off in the café, leaving on the one behind the counter. She locked the front door from the inside and then led Bray out through the kitchen. Milo had his back to them, cleaning the grill. Summer stopped. "Are you sure you won't come for Thanksgiving dinner?" she asked the man.

He half turned. "No, I've got some things to do," he said. "But it means a lot that you'd invite me," he added.

"If you change your mind, just show up. You know we'll have plenty of food," Summer said, opening the back door.

Her red van was parked in the alley next to a big garbage Dumpster. "My car is out front," he said. "Swing around and I'll follow you to Trish's."

"She's just a half mile west of town," Summer said.

Bray waited until Summer had unlocked her door and got in before jogging around the side of the building to his own car. As he turned the corner, his eye automatically scanned the area. The habit had saved his life more than once.

Today, he didn't see anything unusual. Nobody hanging by his car. Nobody across the street, watching the entrance of the café. Nobody...

Wait. The building across the street was a red-brick three-story. On the first floor was an office. Frank Oswald, attorney at law. The windows were dark. Evidently no pressing legal matters to attend to on the afternoon before Thanksgiving.

The second and third floors were apartments

with four large arched windows spread across the face of the building. There it was. Second floor. Second window to the left. A shadow. A man had been standing at the window, watching the café. When Bray had rounded the corner, he'd moved fast, stepping aside, out of view.

Why?

He wanted to pound up the stairs and demand answers. But there was Summer's van. So he ignored his instinct and let the person believe his surveillance had gone undetected.

He got in his car, started it and pulled away from the curb. Summer drove three miles under the speed limit. He wasn't sure if that was normal or whether she was trying to delay the conversation with her children.

Three minutes later, a half mile out of the city limits, Summer put on her left turn signal. She pulled into a long lane that led up to a sprawling brick ranch with a side-load garage with the door up. There was no car.

There was probably an acre of yard and several different gardens that were bare now but would likely be lush with flowers in the spring and summer.

"Sure she's home?" he asked, once he joined Summer at her van.

"Yeah. Her car is in the shop. I'm going to take her to pick it up."

"Nice place."

"It's too big for Trish, but it's the house that she and Rafe bought together. I don't think she can let go of it yet."

A big German shepherd raced around the corner of the house. He stopped short with a low growl when he saw Bray.

The front door of the house opened and Trish stepped outside. Bray would have recognized her anywhere. She still wore her red hair to her waist, as both she and Summer had done in high school.

"Duke," she called. "Settle down. He's a friend." She came off the porch and hugged Bray.

The dog stopped growling, but he looked at Bray with serious black eyes. Bray was confident that if he made one wrong move toward Trish or Summer, the dog would rip him apart.

"It's good to see you," Trish said. "It's been too long."

"I know," he said simply. But because there was no need to dwell on the past, he didn't. "Nice dog," he said. "I hope," he added with a wink.

Trish smiled. "Don't worry about Duke. He was a stray, just showed up one day. But from the minute I took him in, he's been devoted to me. He was super easy to train. Summer's kids adore him."

"How were they?" Summer asked.

"Adie talked nonstop and I got a couple full sentences from Keagan, so I think, overall, it was a pretty great day."

"Good," Summer said.

Trish stared at her sister. "What's wrong? Did something happen at the café?"

Bray wasn't surprised. Trish and Summer had always been in tune with each other. There really was truth to the notion that twins were able to sense things about each other.

"Something weird is going on," Summer said.

Trish said nothing, but Bray could see by the set of her jaw that she was preparing herself for bad news. This was a woman who'd had a few blows already in her life.

"Chief Poole came to see me today. Gary didn't show up for work. And when Daniel Stone went to his house, there were signs that he abruptly left, and a small amount of blood was found at the scene."

"Oh my," Trish said. "Weird and very creepy." She looked over her shoulder as if to verify that the kids were still inside. "I guess it's good that he thought to tell you."

"He was questioning me. I'm a suspect," Summer said.

Trish sucked in a breath. "Of all the stupid, idiotic, senseless—"

"Stop," Summer said.

Bray wanted to smile. In addition to being able

to practically read each other's minds, these two were fiercely protective of each other. He remembered getting his car egged by Trish when she'd seen him with another woman once, not realizing it was a friend of the family he'd picked up from the airport.

"Chief Poole said he might need to talk to the kids. I can't let them get surprised by this."

"Of course not." She turned and took a step toward the house. Then stopped. "What do you think happened to Gary?"

"I have no idea. He's been even more moody than normal lately. But this kind of stuff doesn't happen in Ravesville. I'm scared."

"Did you try his cell phone?"

"I did. Goes right to voice mail."

"He's done this before," Trish said.

"I told Chief Poole that. But this seems different." Summer squared her shoulders. "But I swear to you, if he's somewhere warmer, with a fishing line in the water, I'm going to strangle him with it."

Trish smiled. "I hope you didn't mention that to Chief Poole."

"No. But he probably knows enough about our situation that he wouldn't be surprised."

Trish opened her front door and motioned for Summer and Bray to enter first. She followed them in, with the dog close to her side.

"Hey, guys," Summer said. "Mom's here."

Again, Adie came running around the corner. Bray wondered if the little girl ever walked anywhere. She stopped fast, almost pitching forward, when she saw Bray. "You came back," she said.

He smiled at her. "I did. Remember my name?"

"Bray-Neigh," she said.

"Close enough," he said.

Summer stuck her head around the corner. "Keagan, can I see you for a minute?"

The kid ambled into the kitchen. He wore pajama pants and a faded green T-shirt. "Yeah," he said, ignoring Bray.

"Come here," Summer said to her children. She led them over to the kitchen table and she sat down. She pointed for them to take chairs. "I have something to tell you," she said. "I don't want you to be worried or scared. I *do* want you to understand what's happened."

"What, Mama?" Adie asked.

"This is about your dad. He was expected at work this morning and he didn't show up. Chief Poole is concerned about that."

"Maybe his alarm didn't go off," Keagan said.

"He's not at the house," Summer said. "Do either of you know anything about where your dad may have gone? Did he say anything to you yesterday?"

"He said, ''Bye, Adie,'" the little girl said.

Summer leaned forward and gave her little girl a hug. She looked over Adie's shoulder at her oldest child. "Keagan?"

"He was mad that you weren't there," Keagan said. "Nothing too odd about that."

Bray could tell that it pained Summer to hear her child so coldly remark upon the relationship she had with her ex.

"It's possible," she said, "that Chief Poole might want to talk to you about your dad. All you need to do is tell the truth. Whatever it is, just tell the truth."

"Did something bad happen to Dad?" Keagan asked.

"I don't know," Summer said honestly. "But what I do know is that a lot of good people are concerned about him and doing their very best to find him. I think they will. I do."

Keagan looked at Bray for the first time. "I think it's strange that something happens to my dad the same day you show up."

Bray didn't take offense. In fact, he gave the kid some credit. Hearing that his dad was MIA but still being able to piece together information told him the teen was probably a good thinker.

"Keagan," Summer said, censure in her tone.

Bray waved it away. "I'm a federal agent, Keagan. In New York City. I arrest drug dealers. I'm good at following clues. And I'm going to do everything I can to find your dad."

"Why? You don't even know him."

"You're right. But I've known your mom for a really long time and I'm doing it to help her."

"Whatever," Keagan said. He looked at his mother. "Now what?"

"Now we go on about our lives," she said. "We don't know that something bad has happened to your dad. Everything may be just fine and there's a good explanation for why we can't find him. I don't want you to worry. In fact," she said, looking at Trish, "we have to take Aunt Trish to pick up her car in Hamerton. After that, we can swing by the mall. We need to pick up a few things for Chase and Raney's wedding reception, and I thought we might have dinner at Capaghetti's."

"Spaghetti at Capaghetti's," Adie said in a singsong voice. "And garlic bread. Is Bray-Neigh coming, too?"

Summer looked at him. "Not today, sweetheart," Summer said. "Mr. Hollister is in town to see his family. I'm sure he's anxious to get back to them," she added, definitely letting him know that he wasn't welcome on their little excursion.

Summer's pushing him away was a familiar pain. Trish was frowning at her twin. He understood. It had been the same way fifteen years before, when he'd come back to Ravesville only to learn that Summer had married Gary Blake. When Summer had refused to give him any reasonable explanation, he'd gone to Trish.

"I don't get it," she'd said. "I love you, Bray. You know I do. But she's my sister."

He'd left quietly fifteen years ago. He could do it again. He stood up. "Nice to see you again, Trish," he said.

"You, too," she whispered.

He looked at Summer. "Be careful."

"Go get your things, kids" was all she said.

Chapter Five

Summer drove and Trish rode shotgun. Adie sat in the middle seat and Keagan climbed all the way to the back of the van.

"Bray looks good," Trish said.

Summer checked to make sure both her kids wore their earphones. Bray hadn't looked simply good. He'd looked wonderful. "Yeah."

"No ring," Trish said.

"Nope. He told me he'd never married."

Trish nodded. A few miles went by. "Lousy timing, this thing with Gary."

Summer gave her a sideways glance. "Something may have truly happened to Gary. I don't think we can fault his timing."

"Gary has become such a jerk these past several years that it's hard to care about him," Trish admitted. "Not when I see my sister making the same mistake for a second time."

She didn't have to ask what the mistake was. Trish had always thought she was a fool to marry Gary instead of Bray. It was hard to argue the point. "Trish, I know you mean well, but Bray and I are very different people than we were fifteen years ago. I have two children. An ex-husband. A business. Lots of baggage. He's a single city guy. We're in two different worlds."

"He still looks at you the same way."

Eight simple words. *He still looks at you the same way.* In so many ways, she wanted to be that young girl, the one who had sneaked out of the house so that they could drive out to the old quarry and make love. She'd loved lying close to Bray, feeling his warm skin next to hers, feeling him slip inside her and knowing that nothing could ever come between them.

Until something had. Something bad. "I suppose I should tell Mom about Gary," Summer said. "She might know more about his schedule than the rest of us. She talks to him more often."

"We can swing by her house when we're done at the mall," Trish said. "Are you going to tell her that Bray is back? I think she always liked him."

But she had liked her vodka more. And that had changed the course of all their lives. Her own. Summer's. Bray's. Even Gary's. But Trish didn't know that. It was the only secret that she'd ever kept from her twin.

"I don't see the point," Summer said and turned up the radio.

When they got to the car dealer, Trish went to the service door to pay for her vehicle. Then Summer followed her to the mall. The mall was never not busy, but this afternoon, maybe because people were home getting ready for Thanksgiving Day dinner, it was perhaps less busy. There were actually parking spots.

Inside the sprawling two-story building, Adie skipped along next to her, and Keagan hung back and walked next to Trish. They went to the party store first and bought the decorations they would need for the wedding. Silver and white bows for the tables. Pretty silk flowers in shades of violet and lilac and pale gray. Not necessarily traditional colors for a fall wedding, but when she and Trish had discussed it with Raney and Chase, Raney had seemed to have very definite ideas about the colors. It must have been some kind of inside joke because every time Raney had looked at Chase, as if to check his opinion, he'd simply rolled his eyes and said, "If you love those colors, I'm sure I will, too."

Now, as she and Trish debated over scented or non-scented votive candles, Adie shifted restlessly next to her, anxious to look at the paper-plates-and-napkins aisle. She would be six in three months and was already looking forward to her birthday. For the past two years, it had been all things princess related, and Summer didn't see that changing.

Keagan amused himself looking at the New Year's decorations that had already made their way to the shelves. She knew that he understood much better than his little sister the implications of an adult to suddenly be missing. Adults weren't supposed to do things like that. He was probably worried. She had deliberately not mentioned that there had been blood. That was more than they needed to know at this point, more than they should be expected to handle.

That was why she'd suggested the trip to the mall. Trish had already told her that she'd be happy to get the things they needed. Summer just thought the trip would be a good diversion. Maybe she'd even splurge a little and let them each buy something.

She let Adie lead her to the birthday-party aisle, and they spent the next fifteen minutes picking out the perfect plates and napkins. Then it was time to check out. When they left the store, she hung back, letting Keagan take the lead. He probably wouldn't verbalize what he wanted to do, but he might wander there.

Sure enough, he led them to the small arcade that was at the end of the mall. There were at least twenty kids inside, standing in front of machines. He looked over his shoulder at Summer.

"Thirty minutes," she said. She started to follow him inside, but Trish grabbed her arm. "He's not going to want his mother to be with him," Trish said.

"You're right," Summer admitted.

"Listen, I'll wait outside on this bench. If he tries to leave, I'll tackle him. If there's trouble inside, I'll start cracking heads."

Summer hugged her twin. "You always have my back," she said.

"I know," Trish said, her tone smug. "Going for aunt of the year. Vote early and often."

"I'm going to take Adie to get some shoes. She's growing out of the ones she has on."

"Okay. Leave the other bags here. Once we're done, I'll take Keagan home. How about I get Capaghetti's to go and we forget about Mom for the night. Keagan and I'll meet you at your house."

She would see her mother the next day at Thanksgiving dinner. By then, Gary might be back and they wouldn't even need to have the conversation. "That sounds perfect," she said. Summer grabbed Adie's hand and led her little girl through the busy mall.

When they got to the store, Adie insisted on tie shoes, stating that Velcro was for babies. She tried on at least ten pairs before they found one that fit and was the exact right shade of pink. Summer paid and she let Adie carry the bag. On the way out of the store, she glanced at her watch. Close to five. If she and Adie hurried, they would be home and have a salad made by the time Trish and Keagan arrived with the spaghetti.

They were thirty feet from the exit when she felt someone brush up against her left side. She turned to look, but at the same moment, she was pushed hard. She knocked into Adie and struggled to keep them both from going to the ground.

Furious, she swung around and saw a man, his face partially obscured by the hood of his gray sweatshirt. His arm was close to his body.

He had a gun. And it was pointed at Adie.

"If you scream, I'll shoot her," he said. He nodded his head at a side door. "Step through there. I just want to talk to you about your ex-husband."

Summer could see that none of the other busy shoppers were paying them any attention. Would he really shoot if she screamed? Could she take the chance?

No, she could not.

She gripped Adie's hand even tighter and walked through the door. There, another man stood, his face obscured by a ski mask.

Too late she saw that he had something in his hand.

Oh, Adie, she thought.

WHEN BRAY GOT HOME, Raney and Nalana were in the kitchen. Raney was making a green-bean casserole and Nalana was rolling out pie shells.

"What kind?" he asked, giving them each a quick hug.

"Pumpkin. Any word on the man who is missing?"

"Nope. Not sure if that's good or bad news. Where are my brothers?"

"Tearing out the bath," Raney said, pointing to the hallway that led to the downstairs bedroom and attached bath.

His parents' room. His mother and Brick's room. So many ghosts. "You trust them with a hammer?" he asked.

"More than we trust them with Thanksgiving dinner," Raney said. "Want a drink?"

"I'll get it." He grabbed three beers from the fridge, opened them and carried them to the bedroom. He arrived in time to see his brothers wrestle the double-sink vanity through the bathroom doorway.

"Hey," he said.

Cal spied the beers and smiled. "It's five o'clock somewhere."

"It's practically five o'clock here," Chase said, grabbing one for himself.

Bray looked at his watch. By now, Summer should have finished at the mall and be on her way to eat the spaghetti dinner that Adie had been so excited about.

What kind of Thanksgiving were those kids going to have if their dad didn't show up?

"How was Summer?" Chase asked.

"Holding up pretty well. Chief Poole had already been to see her." Bray took a deep pull on his beer. "What do you think of Gary Blake?" he asked, looking at Chase.

"When I first brought Raney to Ravesville, we had a little trouble. She was run off the road. Blake was the investigating officer. I thought he was a lazy cop. Then later, we learned that it might have been something very different."

"What do you mean?"

"He might have had a reason to brush it under the rug. The description of the car matched one driven by Sheila Stanton."

"The same Sheila Stanton that you dated?" Bray asked.

"The same. But we couldn't prove it. And then we learned that they'd had a thing. But they were quiet about it. It helped us understand why he wasn't interested in arresting her. When we were in St. Louis so that Raney could testify against Harry Malone at his murder trial, we heard that Sheila had left town rather unexpectedly."

"So he's nursing a broken heart?" Bray asked.

"Broken heart. Bruised pride. Something in between," Chase said. "Don't feel sorry for him. He's a small-town cop with a big ego that gets in the way of him doing the right thing. I don't think he's got a whole lot of friends here."

"So there are plenty of people who think he's a horse's ass. That's not generally enough to get you in trouble."

Chase set his beer down. "I'm not sure if I should say anything, but given what almost happened yesterday, I think you should know. More than a month ago, Raney happened to see a big bruise on Summer's back. When she asked Summer about it, she got the impression that Summer didn't want anybody to know about it. I don't know if it was Gary Blake."

"It was," Bray said. "Summer ended up on the wrong end of his boot."

Cal set his beer down. "She told you that?"

Bray nodded.

"And you're sure you didn't kill Gary Blake last night?" Cal asked.

Bray shook his head. "I thought about it. Went to his house and knocked on the door. Nobody answered. I guess that gave me enough time to channel my anger in a more manageable direction."

"You didn't tell Chief Poole that," Chase said. "If he finds out that you were at Blake's house, he's going to have more questions."

"I guess I'll deal with that at the time," Bray

said. "There's no evidence connecting me to a crime. I didn't do anything." He finished his beer and walked over to look at the paint can that was sitting near the bathroom door. "'Snapdragon in Splendor.' What the hell kind of color is that?"

Chase shrugged. "Talk to Raney," he said. "I just put it on the walls."

Cal put down his empty bottle. "I've got to get going," he said. "I told Gordy Fitzler that Nalana and I'd be there by six."

"Old Man Fitzler?"

"Yeah. He's selling his house. Nalana and I looked at it the other day. We want it. His daughters are home for the holiday and he wants to make sure they're okay with the decision."

With his index finger, Bray pointed at his brothers. "You two? Both staying in Ravesville? Living down the road from each other?"

Cal smiled. "Makes it easy to borrow a cup of sugar."

Something had definitely happened here. He chose his words carefully. "I'm glad that the two of you feel comfortable borrowing sugar from each other. That's a nice change."

"The best," Chase said.

"It's important to know that there's always… sugar close by," Cal added.

Yes, it was. "But how does staying in Ravesville work with your jobs?" Bray asked Cal.

"Well, Nalana was evidently so highly valued that when she told her bosses that she intended to quit so that she could live with me in Ravesville, her bosses were quick to offer up an alternative that will allow her to remain with the FBI but work remotely, as long as she's willing to travel some."

"And for you?" Bray asked.

"I'm not interested in being in another country if Nalana is here. I'm setting up a little engineering shop in the outbuilding at my new house. I know a thing or two about ships and submarines and just maybe have an idea or two of how to make a better flyswatter."

"Sounds about perfect for a formal navy SEAL with a mechanical-engineering degree." Bray turned to Chase. "How about you? This remodeling can't keep you busy forever."

"Thank the good Lord for that," Chase said, draining his beer. "I'll stay on the job with the St. Louis police department for now. They're going to work with me and try to group my shifts together so that I work three on and four off one week and four on and three off the following week. That way I'll have seven days off in the middle of every two weeks to be here. I've still got my condo and can stay in St. Louis when I need to. And Raney, well, there is a lot to do on the house yet and she's really good at that. Plus, we're hoping to start a family quickly." He looked at his brothers. "I never saw myself as a dad, and suddenly, I can't see myself as anything else."

The three men looked at one another. They were brothers who had lost their own father too early. "You'll make a great one," Bray said.

He turned when he heard footsteps coming down the hall. Raney and Nalana entered.

"What's going on?" Raney asked, looking at Chase first, then Cal.

Chase smiled. "Bray was admiring your paint choices."

Raney sighed. "Sticks and stones," she said breezily as if discussions about paint colors were old stuff to her.

"We were talking about sugar—you know, how much you need for baking and…other stuff," Cal added.

Nalana wrinkled her nose. "You don't bake," she said.

Cal shrugged. "Yes, but I did say I'd cook the turkey tomorrow. I'm looking forward to dinner. It's got to be better here than on a mountain in Afghanistan. That's where I was last year at this time. Let me tell you, a turkey MRE leaves a lot to be desired."

"Hard to argue that," Bray said. Even though he was unsettled about how he'd left Summer, he was happy to be here with his brothers and the women who were important to them.

His phone rang. Speaking of Summer. "Hi," he said.

"Bray," she said, her voice thick with tears. "I need you."

"Honey," he said, already moving. "What's wrong?"

"They took Adie. She's gone."

Chapter Six

"Who took her?" he demanded, his heart starting to beat fast.

"I don't know. Two men."

"Where?"

"At the mall."

"Have you contacted the police?"

"I can't," she said. "They put a rag over my mouth and knocked me out with something. I don't think I was out for very long, but when I woke up, Adie and both the men were gone. They left a note."

"What did it say?"

"'Don't tell the police or anyone else. If you do, you'll never see your daughter again.' Oh, Bray, what am I going to do?"

"You did the right thing. You called me. Now where are you?"

"In my car. About five miles from the mall. I was shaking so much I couldn't drive. I pulled off. I'm at a gas station at the intersection of Highway 8 and Sycamore Road."

"Is anybody watching you? Were you followed?"

She didn't answer right away. "I don't think so," she said. "Nobody seems to be paying any attention to me."

"Okay. Stay there. Lock your doors. Don't get out of the car. I'll be there as soon as I can."

She didn't say anything.

"Summer," he said, his tone firm. "Promise me that you'll do what I asked."

"I promise," she said.

"Did you tell Trish?"

"Not yet," she wailed. "Oh, God, what am I going to tell Keagan?"

"We'll figure it out. I'm on my way." He disconnected the phone and turned to his family. "Summer's five-year-old daughter has been kidnapped."

Raney and Nalana both gasped. Chase and Cal gathered their women close.

"What's your plan?" Cal asked, his voice calm.

"She was warned not to call the police. So we won't. For the time being. But we need access to info that the police could normally provide. They took her from the mall in Hamerton. There's got to be video surveillance of the parking lot, the entrances and the interior hallways."

Nalana stepped forward. "On it. I work with a guy who can tap into any system known to man. He'll be able to get it."

Bray nodded.

"Do you think this has anything to do with Gary Blake's disappearance?" Chase asked.

"I don't know, but I think it's a hell of a coincidence, and I don't much believe in coincidence. Summer's son and sister could also be at risk."

"Raney and I'll take that one," Chase said. "We won't leave their side. You want us to tell Trish what's going on?"

"Yeah, but not Keagan." Summer would want to tell her baby rock.

Bray swung his gaze to Cal. "Can you follow me in your car? Once we get more details from Summer, I'm going to want you to go to the mall and look for physical evidence."

Cal fished his keys out of his pocket. "Let's roll."

Bray pulled his Glock 27 out of the holster on his belt. He had, of course, flown with his gun, but with a very limited amount of ammunition. He looked at his brothers. "Do you have some ammo that I can have?"

"Absolutely," Chase said. "It'll just take me a minute. It's upstairs."

While Chase was gone, Raney left the room

and came back with two high-powered flashlights. "These might come in handy," she said.

They would. And when Chase came in moments later with enough ammo to defend a small city, he was struck by the knowledge of how important family was at a time like this. You could count on them.

He was almost out the door when Nalana came running toward him, carrying a soft blanket. "For Adie," she said, "when you find her."

BRAY DROVE VERY FAST, and his mind was going even faster. His car was too quiet and it allowed his mind to shift into dangerous territory. Blame. He should have gone with Summer to the mall, whether he was invited or not. He should have realized Blake's disappearance might mean something more, that Summer and her children were at risk.

But knowing that there was little to be gained by would-have, should-have games, he forced himself to focus on more productive thoughts.

Was it possible that Summer and Adie had simply been in the wrong place at the wrong time? That the kidnapping was random, not associated with them specifically? That the kidnappers had chosen the mall as a likely place to be able to play grab-and-run with a child?

Possible but doubtful. Much more likely that

Adie had been the target and the mall had presented the best opportunity. They hadn't hurt Summer. The thought that they could just as easily have put a knife in her back or a bullet in her head made him almost need to roll down his window and get sick.

When he reached the gas station, he saw Summer's car. She was sitting in the driver's seat, staring straight ahead. He drove around the perimeter of the gas station twice before pulling into a spot next to her.

He saw Cal pull into one of the bays and get gas. Unless someone knew them well, nobody would guess that they were together.

He opened his door and heard the *click* of Summer's passenger door unlocking. He opened the door and slid in.

She looked terrified. He wanted to take her into his arms and promise her that everything would be okay.

Instead, he reached over, laid a hand on her thigh. "We'll get her back," he said.

"What kind of monsters steal a child, Bray? What kind?" she asked, her voice breaking.

The worst kind. But there was nothing to be gained by saying that. She already knew that. "Tell me again what happened."

"Adie needed shoes. Trish said that she'd take Keagan home. We bought the shoes and we were walking toward an exit when a man bumped into me. He had a gun. Said he wanted to ask me something about Gary."

"What?" he said sharply. This was new information. He made an effort to gentle his voice. "Try to remember exactly what he said."

"I don't know exactly, but it was something like, 'I want to ask you a question about your ex-husband.'"

Well, that settled that. It was not a random kidnapping. They had known Summer. And this definitely had something to do with her ex.

"Then he said if I didn't do what he said, he'd… he'd shoot Adie."

"You did the right thing."

She shook her head. "My daughter is gone. How could I have done the right thing?"

She was playing the blame game, too. "You couldn't take the chance," he said. "Have you ever seen this man before?"

"No."

"Describe him."

"Late forties, early fifties. White. Very pale skin. Big nose. Brown hair combed to the side, I think. He wore a gray sweatshirt with the hood up. I couldn't see a lot of his face."

"That's okay," he said. She'd been terrified but she was remembering important details. He glanced in the side mirror. Cal was washing his windshield. Nobody else seemed to be paying any attention to them. "Anything else?"

"Taller than me. Probably close to six feet. His pants were dark. But his shoes were light. White athletic shoes."

"Anything about his voice? Accent? Odd cadence?"

She shook her head. "Not really. He sounded… sort of like you. Like he might have lived on the East Coast for a while."

"Did you see his gun? Can you describe it?"

"I saw it. I don't know anything about guns. It was black. Seemed big. He…he had on gloves. They were black, too. Under them, I could see the shape of a big ring on his left hand."

"Okay. What happened after he threatened Adie?"

"He pushed me through a set of double doors that led to a hallway and an exit."

He held up a hand, stopping her. "What part of the mall? Where are the doors located?"

"The southeast end, near Penney's. Just past the toy store. I remember because I was hoping Adie wouldn't ask to go inside. I was hurrying to get home."

"What happened when you went through the doors?"

"There was another man standing there. He had on a ski mask."

"Tell me about him."

She closed her eyes. "Dark clothes. I couldn't see his face or hair, but his eyes were blue. Light blue."

"Probably Caucasian," Bray said. "Height and weight?"

"Shorter than the other guy but still taller than me. So maybe five-nine, five-ten. Stocky. Or maybe just his coat made him look that way. It was a puffy one. Dark. Black or blue."

"Did he talk?"

"No. He's the one who covered my mouth with a rag."

"What else?" Bray prompted.

"When I woke up, Adie was gone. They left this." Holding an envelope by its edge, she handed it to him.

Don't call the police if you ever want to see your daughter again.

The note was on the back side of an envelope, handwritten, printed, all capital letters. Blue ink. "Recognize the writing?" Bray asked, knowing it was a long shot.

"No." She turned in her seat. "Bray, I don't know what to do," she said. "Every minute that goes by, Adie could be in more danger. Hurting."

Her pretty eyes filled with tears. "Should I go to the police?"

"I don't think so," he said. "I don't think you're being watched. Which makes me believe that they've got another way to know if you go to the police."

"But…" Her voice trailed off. "Are you suggesting that the police are involved?"

He shrugged. "I don't know who's involved. But this seems to have something to do with your husband, and he's a cop. Our job is to try to draw logical conclusions based on what we know."

"I can't be logical. I can't even think."

He studied her. "Listen, I have to ask. Do you think it's possible that your ex staged all of this—his disappearance, Adie's kidnapping. Could this be an end run to avoid a potential custody battle?"

"I've never threatened to take the kids away from Gary. Just the opposite. He's the one who cancels his weekends or brings them back early."

Bray pulled his phone from his pocket. He dialed Cal. When his brother answered, he succinctly gave him the location of the abduction and a description of both men. Cal promised to be in touch.

"Who was that?" Summer asked.

"Cal. He's been here the whole time. I want him to go to the mall, see if there's any physical evidence at the scene. Make a few discreet inquiries."

"I appreciate his help," she said.

"The whole family is in on it. Nalana is reaching out to an FBI contact to get the video footage of the mall, and Raney and Chase are going to tell Trish and stay with her and Keagan, just in case."

He could tell by the look on her face that she understood what he was saying. They all needed to be careful.

"I need to tell my mother," she said.

"We will. Is she still in Ravesville?"

"Yes. Still at the old house."

"Okay. Here's what we're going to do. You're going to drive back to the mall and park the van in the lot. Then we'll take my car."

"Why?"

"This red van sticks out like a sore thumb. If we plan on sneaking up on anything, I'd feel better in my bland rental." Plus, if they'd planted some kind of tracking device on the van, he didn't want to make it easy for them.

"It's just so crazy. If these men know Gary then they know that I'm a part owner of a small business. Everybody knows that's not terribly lucrative. I don't have money for a ransom."

"Is it possible that you have something else of value?"

She turned her head. "Like what?"

"I don't know. Something of your ex's."

"I can't imagine. He's been out of the house for over two years. His stuff is gone."

"Some information?"

"Gary and I don't chat a lot. If we talk, it's about the kids. Never his work." She glanced at her cell phone, which was sitting on the middle console. "I don't have a home phone. They need to call my cell." She paused. "They didn't ask me for my phone number."

"They could get it from your ex," he said.

She nodded. "Then why the hell don't they call?" she asked, her tone angry. "That's what kidnappers do, right? They call. They make a demand."

He'd been a beat cop before he'd gone to work at the DEA. Had never worked a kidnapping case, but he was pretty sure that Adie hadn't been snatched for a big ransom. There might not be a call. But he wasn't taking her hope away from her. "We'll be ready when it comes. I promise you," he said. He put his hand on the door. "Are you confident that you can drive?"

"Yes," she said. "I'll park in the lot by Penney's."

He got out and waited while she pulled out of the lot. Then he fell in behind her. She drove much faster than she had the day before, and in just minutes, they were back at the mall. She got out of her van, then stopped, reached back inside and pulled out a bag.

"Adie's shoes," she said, getting into his car. "I…I want her to have them right away when we find her."

Her voice had cracked at the end. And he knew that she was a hair away from unraveling. It made his own heart hurt. The men who'd done this were going to be very, very sorry. He was going to make sure of that.

When they pulled up in front of the two-story on Elmwood Street, Bray saw that her mother had painted the house at some point. It used to be white. Now it was yellow. The old garage that sat behind the house had been torn down and a new one put up. The door was up and he could see an older Ford parked inside. "That your mom's car?"

Summer nodded. "She's always leaving the door up. I've told her a hundred times to make sure she puts it down. She's always telling me to quit worrying, that nothing bad ever happens in Ravesville." Summer turned to him, her expression bleak. "I guess she can't say that anymore."

Something horrible had happened. To her granddaughter. Bray reached out his arm, put two fingers under Summer's chin. "We're going to get Adie back. You have to stay positive."

"Thank you," she whispered. "Thank you for being here, for being somebody that I knew I could call, that I knew would help me. It's more than I deserve after…everything."

Now was not the time for questions, not the time to ask why she hadn't waited for him. "I'm not going anywhere," he said.

Chapter Seven

Wednesday, 6:00 p.m.

Summer didn't bother to knock. "Mom," she called out as she opened the door.

"In the kitchen."

They walked down the short hallway. Flora Wright was at her stove, stirring a pot of something. She turned, her spoon in the air.

The years had been kind to Flora Wright. Her brown hair was streaked with gray and there were lines on her face that hadn't been there fifteen years ago. But all in all, better than what he'd expected. Flora had been a hard drinker, and in a small town, the talk had been inevitable. Bray had heard it. His parents, too. His mom had been smart enough to tell him to make his own decisions about a person's worth and not let someone else do it for him.

He'd told Summer to ignore it and she'd done her best, but he'd always known that it was a source of embarrassment to her. Trish had simply been angry about it, and that had caused a lot of tension in the Wright house, with Summer smack-dab in the middle as peacemaker.

He was pretty confident Summer's mom had given up the bottle. Good for her. "Hi, Flora," he said.

"Bray." Her smile was genuine. "I heard you were back for your brother's wedding." She turned to her daughter. "What's wrong?" she asked immediately.

"Someone took Adie," Summer said.

The spoon hit the tile floor with a clatter. "What?" Flora asked, putting her hand on the counter, as if to steady herself.

Summer told her mother about the mall and then about Gary, too. By the time she was finished, Flora was tight-lipped and pale.

"What do we do?" she asked.

"We wait," Summer said. "But in the meantime, Mom, can you think of anything about Gary that would help us understand why he might have suddenly disappeared?"

"He hasn't been happy since the divorce," Flora said.

There was a look exchanged between mom and daughter that he couldn't decipher. Had Flora been upset about the divorce? Any parent probably would be, especially because there were children involved. But it seemed like something more.

"It's been two years, Mom," Summer said. "Why now?"

"He's been out of town a lot these last couple months," Flora said.

How would she know? The question must have been in his eyes, because she shrugged and said, "He pays me to clean his house. It's hardly been dirty."

"You never mentioned that you were cleaning his house," Summer said, her voice tight.

"I clean houses, Summer. You know that."

"But... Never mind—it's not important," Summer said, waving a hand.

Bray was glad that she was staying focused, but certainly the relationship between Gary Blake and his ex-mother-in-law was interesting. "Do you have a key to his house?" Bray asked.

Flora nodded. "For the kitchen door. What are you going to do?"

"Search it. There's got to be a clue somewhere that can lead us to Adie."

Flora pulled a silver key off her key ring. "What should I do?"

"I'll call my brother Chase. He'll be in touch."

"How you holding up?" Bray asked when they were back in his car.

She was petrified. "Fine," she said.

He nodded. "Your mom looks good."

She understood the subtext. "She stopped drinking fifteen years ago."

"Must have been a big year."

She turned her head.

"That's the year you married Blake."

He was getting too close. She needed to change the subject. "Chief Poole may have somebody watching Gary's house."

"We won't get caught," he said confidently.

She needed to draw upon that confidence. Maybe it would leak over and she'd feel more in control. Adie had now been gone for an hour. And no word from anybody.

She gave him directions to Gary's house. It was at the edge of town, one block off the main street. He'd been renting it since the divorce. The owners were both in a nursing home and their son was grateful to have Gary in the house. He might not feel the same if it came to light that something bad had happened to Gary there. People were superstitious in small towns, and it might make it hard to ultimately sell the property.

It seemed impossible that it had just been this morning that Chief Poole had come to the café and told her that Gary was missing. Once the chief had given her details, she'd understood the seriousness of the situation. But before that, when he'd simply said he was missing, her very first thought had been relief. The interaction with Gary at the church had been so charged with unexpected anger. She simply wasn't up to dealing with that again. Especially not with Bray in town.

"It's down this street," she said.

Bray didn't turn. Kept going straight. Turned at the next street instead. "How many houses in?" he asked.

"Five." They drove another hundred feet. "It's the two-story colonial. You can see the roofline from here."

Bray pulled the car over and killed his lights. "So his backyard butts up to this house's backyard?" he asked, pointing at a smaller brick Cape Cod.

"Yes."

"Okay. This is the way to go in. Maybe you should stay here," he said.

"No," she said simply. Not an option. She might not have a right to be in Gary's house, but she was the one with the key. She would not let Bray take this risk alone.

She grabbed a flashlight and opened her door, causing Bray to hurry to catch up with her. He carried a flashlight in one hand and his gun in the other. "Keep your light off for now," he whispered. "We'll only turn it on if we absolutely have to."

Her eyes adjusted to the dark, and she was able to see enough that she didn't trip and fall. Someone in the neighborhood had lit their fireplace. A comfortable smell, so at odds with the terror that was flowing through her veins.

As they walked through the neighbor's yard and into Gary's backyard, she prayed that a dog wouldn't suddenly alert the neighborhood to their presence. Or take a bite out of them. But the night stayed quiet. "This is it," she said.

Bray turned on his flashlight, keeping it mostly pointed at the ground. "Big house for a single guy," he said softly.

"Not a lot of rental property in Ravesville. I think he took what he could get. That door there leads to the kitchen. It's the one that wasn't closed tight."

"Chief Poole told you that?"

"Yes. Not you?"

Bray shook his head. "Probably didn't think I needed the details." He paused. "Maybe he thought I knew them," he added.

It was very dark in the backyard. Street side, it would be different because there were lights on the corners of each block. It had been a good idea to come this way.

The house was completely dark. They approached and Summer handed Bray the key. Then she held the flashlight while he unlocked the door. When he opened the door and used the tail of his shirt to wipe off any prints, the enormity of what they were doing settled down upon her.

They were disturbing what might be a crime scene. But she kept going, knowing she would do far worse to get Adie back.

She had, of course, been to Gary's house several times, dropping off and picking up the kids. She knew her way around the downstairs. The kitchen had a bath and laundry room off to one side. Then there was a family room and a formal dining room that had been empty of furniture since the day Gary moved in. The son had left everything except for the dining room set, because he needed one.

The milk and the cereal bowl that the chief had described were still on the table. She pointed to them. "This is Chief Poole's evidence of a quick departure."

Bray flicked his flashlight toward the floor, then the back door. "And that's the blood."

It looked like a smear of brown dirt on the back of the cream-colored wood.

"What are we looking for?" she asked.

"I don't know. Just keep your eyes open for anything that looks odd or interesting." As they walked from the kitchen to the family room, he pointed at the closed drapes and said, "We got lucky. Still, be careful with your flashlight and don't turn on any other lights."

After a quick search of the downstairs didn't net anything of value, they took the steps. She had never been in the upstairs. There were two bedrooms across from a bath. The first one was Adie's. There was a chest of drawers and a bed, with two dolls that she'd taken from home perched against the pillows.

Waiting. For Adie to come and play.

Summer covered her mouth. Where was her child?

She forced herself to move on. The next bedroom had to be where Keagan slept, but one wouldn't have been able to tell. There was nothing of the boy in the room.

The bath across the hall was clean. Her mother had probably seen to that. Her mother cleaned houses four days a week and generally told her, in excruciating detail, about each house. But she had never once mentioned that she was cleaning Gary's. She'd probably expected that Summer wouldn't be happy about it.

She didn't care. Her mother could have lunch with Gary every day for all it mattered to her.

At the end of the hall was the master suite, with a big bedroom and an attached bath. In the corner of the master was a big desk. If the kids' rooms had been sterile, this was the exact opposite. There were dirty clothes on the floor, piles of newspapers at the end of the bed, a pile of what might be clean yet unfolded laundry on the dresser and several take-out food bags crumpled up in the garbage can in the corner. There were two more on the floor nearby as if Gary had been eating in bed and tossed the bag but hadn't quite hit the mark. The room smelled of old greasy French fries and onions.

Something told her that Gary had instructed her mother to leave his room alone. She picked her way around the debris on the floor. He needed to be a little less protective of his man cave and a little more hygienic.

The only thing that seemed orderly in the whole room was the desk in the corner. It was clear with the exception of a spiral notebook and two pens, both from the Wright Here, Wright Now Café.

Bray followed her over. With the tips of his fingers, he picked up the notebook, ran his thumb along the edges to see the pages. Then again. They were all blank. He put the notebook down.

Then he knelt. His fingertips again protected by his shirttail, he opened the three drawers on the one side of the desk. Pens, paper clips and rubber bands in the top. A stack of unused file folders in the middle. And in the bottom, a plastic bin marked "Insurance." Bray opened it up and there was a stack of Explanation of Benefit forms.

"He covers the kids," Summer said.

Bray closed the bin and shoved it back in the drawer. "Nothing here," he said. "Does the desk seem unusually clean?" he asked.

"Given the rest of the room, yes. But Gary has always been tidy with paperwork."

"But no bank statements, no credit-card bills, no tax returns. Absolutely nothing financial."

She tried to remember where Gary had kept those things when they'd been married. They'd had a joint checking account where paychecks got automatically deposited. Statements had come to the house and been filed somewhere in the office that sat next to their family room. Bills had come in the mail. And he'd paid them. It had been his task, the way cooking dinner was her task.

"He was switching over, doing lots of things electronically. Everyone has been, right? It's easier. Better for the environment."

"Maybe he's green down to his shorts. Or maybe he didn't want to take the chance that his ex-mother-in-law would stick her nose where it didn't belong." Bray walked over toward the walk-in closet.

Summer followed. It was half-empty, reminding her that Gary had never been a clotheshorse. He'd worn a uniform every day, so there wasn't a big need to have a lot of clothes. There were some dress pants and maybe five shirts. Several extra uniforms.

Bray pushed clothing out of the way so that he could see the shelves behind them. A few books, a stack of car magazines. Bray systematically shook each one, to see if something would fall out.

They were just about to back out of the closet when Summer saw the lizard-print cowboy boots. She could never remember seeing Gary wear boots of any kind, let alone boots like this.

It was enough to make her reach for them. To make her pick one up. She dumped it on end. Nothing. Did the same with the other boot. Nothing there, either. Was just about to put them back when she decided to stick her hand inside.

And that was when she felt it. A key, taped to the inside top of the boot. She pulled, and key and tape came together.

"What's that to?" Bray asked.

She looked at it, saw the engraving. "It's from a bank in St. Louis. Maybe for a safe-deposit box." She looked up at Bray. "Gary and I never had a safe-deposit box at a bank in St. Louis. At least I don't think we did."

Bray looked at his watch. "I want to know what's in that box, but it's six thirty on the Wednesday before Thanksgiving. The banks are probably all closed."

Summer shook her head. "Not necessarily. Some of the banks have started offering extended banking hours," she said. "As late as eight or nine o'clock at night. The competition is fierce."

He took another look at the key, then pulled his

smartphone from his pocket and punched buttons. In just minutes, he was dialing. "Can you tell me how late you're open?" he asked.

"Eight," he repeated, probably for her benefit. "Thank you," he said and hung up.

"This is terrific," she said. "Let's go."

"We're an hour and a half from the city. In good traffic. Plus, we have a key, but if your name's not on the list, you won't be able to get into it."

He was right. She needed to think. There was really only one option. "You can pretend you're Gary."

"They aren't going to take my word for it. They'll ask for identification."

"I have his passport. I found it recently. We got it when we went to Mexico for a vacation. I think he forgot about it. I remember that his picture wasn't great—a little blurry. His hair was longer then, not the length of yours, but maybe, if someone doesn't look too close, you could pass for him."

He didn't look convinced. She knew it was a long shot, but what other leads did they have? "We have to try," she added.

"It's going to add another ten minutes to run by your house to get his passport," he said, already moving toward the stairs.

"We have to make it," she said, running to catch up. "The banks will all be closed tomorrow."

BRAY PUSHED HIS rental to ninety and moved in and out of the traffic that was on Interstate 44. Thankfully, traffic was light on the highway. They didn't talk.

Summer stared straight ahead, glancing every few minutes at her phone perched on the console between them. Twenty minutes into the trip, a phone rang and she jumped.

It was his cell phone. Cal. He put it on speaker. "Yeah," he said.

"I checked the hallway at the mall and it was clean, except there was a receipt, folded and wrinkled, as if it might have come out of a pocket accidentally."

Like maybe when somebody pulled their gloves out of their pocket. "For?" Bray asked.

"A gas station in St. Louis. Purchase was made earlier this afternoon, for forty-two gallons."

"Forty-two," Bray repeated. "Are they driving a semi?"

"I checked the price. Matches up to regular unleaded. Not diesel."

"I guess we look for vehicles with a big tank," Bray said.

"We can maybe do better. Nalana is going to have her guy try to get into the security tapes from the gas station," Cal said.

"Did he get anything from the mall?"

"Yeah. We're sorting through it now."

"Okay. Call me when you've got something," Bray said. "We're on our way to St. Louis to look at a safe-deposit box."

"Good luck," Cal said and hung up.

"It's something," Summer said after a long pause.

"Bits and pieces. That's how most crimes are solved. Rarely is there a big reveal. It's more often a process of paying attention to everything and sorting through what is important and what isn't."

Again she was silent for a long moment. "What if that takes too long?" she asked finally.

He didn't have an answer for that. "After we go to the bank, I want you to eat something," he said, changing the subject.

She shrugged. "I'm not sure I can."

"You need to," he said. "You never ate lunch."

"I was already planning the trip to Capaghetti's."

Her day had turned out very differently than she'd planned. Wasn't that the way it always worked? The things you worried about rarely happened and then, out of nowhere, you'd be slapped upside the head with something out of left field. Car accidents. Brain tumors. Little kids with handguns. He glanced at his left shoulder. Only time he'd ever taken a bullet had been from a ten-year-old. He'd been busting the kid's father when the kid had crawled out from under the bed with a .38. He'd managed to stay standing long enough to keep the dad subdued and he'd got an attaboy from his boss for having the wherewithal not to return fire.

When life tossed you lemons, you tossed 'em right back. Only choice you had. You kept going.

"You have to eat," he said. "You need to stay strong."

"Stay? I'm not strong," she argued.

"Don't underestimate yourself. You're a single parent with two kids and you have your own business."

"Not strong in the ways that count," she said.

He waited for her to continue, but that appeared to be all she was willing to say. She was probably stronger than she thought. At least he hoped she was. She was going to need to be. He glanced at his watch. They were making good time. Even if they hit some traffic closer to the city, they should be okay.

He looked at Gary Blake's passport that Summer had tossed onto the dash. She'd been right. The quality of the picture wasn't great. Plus, the man's straight hair had been unkempt and shaggy around his face. When Bray had looked at it, he'd pulled the rubber band out of the short ponytail that he pulled his hair back into when he wasn't working.

"I suppose you can't do anything about your cheekbones," Summer said.

He'd got the clean lines of his face from his mother. Blake's face was rounder. "Nope."

"It'll be okay," she said, looking at the clock on the dash.

He hoped so. He reached for the passport again and opened it. This time, with one eye on the road and one on the page, he studied the signature. Tight, cramped script. Small loop in the *Y*. The *E* at the end of *Blake* was just a line. "Okay. I'll practice at the stoplights once we get to St. Louis."

"It's a crime to impersonate someone to gain access to their bank records?" Her tone had changed. A half hour ago she'd been full speed ahead, and now she sounded as if she were putting on the brakes.

"Yes," he said.

"Gary's the type that might not take it well."

"Even if I'm doing it for him. For his child."

"He hates you."

That surprised him. He knew why he hated Blake, but what kind of beef could he have with Bray? He'd won. He'd got the girl. "Why?"

"I don't know," she said quickly. "But you're taking a risk. Too big a risk." She paused. "It could be your career. It's too much to ask. I'll find another way."

"You're not asking," he said. "I'm volunteering. You're right. We need to know what's in that box. And we need to know it quickly. Focus on that. Nothing else."

He saw her swallow hard. But she didn't argue. Ten miles went by before she turned to him. "Why don't they call, Bray? Why the hell hasn't anyone called?"

"I don't know," he said. "But we won't stop until we find her. We won't."

The traffic got heavier as they got closer to St. Louis. He could see Summer looking at the clock on the dash every few minutes. He drove fast, speeding up to avoid red lights. He was not going to have this woman have to wait days to see what was in that damn box.

He saw the big bank at the corner and took the first parking spot he could find. He took one more glance at the signature and shoved the passport into his pocket.

He opened his car door. "Come on, honey. It's showtime."

Chapter Eight

Wednesday, 7:53 p.m.

The bank had big heavy doors, shiny marble-looking floors and a security guard standing near a flagpole. Summer forced herself to slow down to a walk and she pasted a smile on her face.

"Good evening," she said.

The man nodded.

There was a row of teller bays but only two were open. Young girls, no older than twenty-five, were manning them. It made sense. New hires would be working the night before Thanksgiving. Those with greater seniority were home defrosting the turkey and making pie.

She could only hope the staffing pattern continued through to the safe-deposit-box area.

Off to the left was customer service. It was dark.

Beyond that, there was a sign on the wall. Safe-Deposit Boxes.

There was a desk and one of those rope things that they used at concerts and similar events to keep the crowd back. But there was no crowd. Not even anyone at the desk.

As she and Bray walked toward the sign, one of the young women behind the teller counter started toward them.

"Can I help you?" she asked. Her name badge said Treena.

Bray nodded in her direction. "I'm Gary Blake and I need to take a look at something in my box."

"Oh, sure," she said. Treena seemed to be looking over their shoulders as if expecting reinforcements to appear. But then she gave a little shrug and sat at the desk.

She tapped on the keyboard of the desktop computer. The screen came alive. "You said your name was Blake," she said.

"Gary Blake," Bray said pleasantly.

She keyed it in. Then looked up. "Do you have your key?"

Bray held it up.

"I'll need to see a picture ID," she said.

"Of course." Bray pulled out the passport and handed it to her. She opened it, looked at the picture.

Looked up at Bray.

He didn't flinch.

Treena looked across the bank. At what, Summer had no idea. She could feel the breath in her lungs. Burning.

Treena looked at Bray one more time, then the passport picture.

"It's a terrible photo, isn't it?" Summer said, moving a step forward. "I kept telling my husband to get a haircut."

Treena turned to Summer. "Are you Mrs. Blake?"

"I am," Summer said. "But I'm not on the box," she said, as if she knew that to be true.

"That's right. But if you had some identification you could show me, that would be helpful."

Summer opened her purse. Her license, anything of importance, said Summer Wright. Opposite of helpful.

She unfolded her billfold and pulled out her library card. It was more than five years old but had her picture and, more important, had her name as Summer Blake.

Treena looked at it and smiled. "Thank you." She used a swipe card that hung on a lanyard around her neck to open the glass door that led back to the safe-deposit boxes. "Follow me, Mr. Blake," she said.

Summer walked over to the waiting area and sank down in one of the leather chairs, just seconds before she was sure that her knees were going to give out. She looked at the clock on the wall. Seven fifty-seven.

Three minutes to spare.

She felt as if she might throw up, and she was grateful that she hadn't eaten for many hours.

It was five and a half minutes later that Bray came through the glass door followed by Treena. He was not carrying anything.

Summer could barely contain her disappointment.

"Thank you," Bray said from somewhere far away.

"You're welcome, Mr. Blake. You two have a nice Thanksgiving," she said.

Adie loved pumpkin pie with more whipped cream than pie. Oh, God. She felt dizzy.

"You, too," Bray said. He stood in front of Summer's chair, held out a hand. "Let's go, honey."

When she didn't move, he pulled her from the chair and put his arm under her elbow and steered her toward the door. "Hang on," he whispered, no hesitation in his stride.

Now what? It was all she could think. Now what would she do to find her baby?

She heard the security guard locking the door behind them. Forced one foot in front of the other.

With his hand still cupped around her elbow, he steered her back to the car. He opened the passenger side and gently pushed her in. Then he was around the car. Inside.

"Are you okay?" he asked.

She was never going to be okay again. "Yes," she lied. He'd told her that she was strong. She'd better start trying to prove him right.

He unzipped his jacket and pulled out a handful of 8.5-by-11 lined sheets of paper, folded over. Maybe eight or ten. She looked closer. They were likely from the spiral notebook on the top of Gary's desk.

"The only thing in the box was these," Bray said. "I didn't take time to look at them."

She made some sound at the back of her throat. Something short of a sob. She'd been so sure that there was nothing. She reached for the papers.

"Keep them in order," Bray said, "in case that means something, and only touch them by the edges."

The pages were mostly blank. Except that each one, in the middle of the page, had one line of numbers. She quickly flipped pages. There were eleven of them. "What is this?" she cried. "What the hell is this?"

"I don't know."

She pressed her hand against her forehead. The headache that had been lurking ever since that man had put something over her mouth threatened to take her under.

She shoved the papers back at Bray. They did her no good anyway. Did Adie no good.

"It's obviously in code," Bray said. "We have to figure it out."

"That could take days," she said.

He started the car.

"Where are we going?"

"Back to Ravesville. We need Cal and Nalana to help us. Maybe Chase, Raney and your sister, too. The more eyes the better."

"My mother is a wiz at crossword puzzles. I know it's not the same, but she's good at figuring things out."

"Her, too. I got a text from Chase earlier. He and Raney brought Trish, Keagan and your mom to his house." He slowed for a red light, but when there was no traffic coming, he didn't stop.

It was fifteen minutes before she voiced what she'd been thinking since Bray had first pulled the papers from inside his coat. "This cannot be good for Gary. He's into something bad, isn't he?"

"Looks like it," Bray said. "But until we figure out the code, we won't know. Maybe not even then. But that can't be our focus. Our focus is on finding Adie."

He understood. He really did. "Why didn't you marry, Bray? Why didn't you marry and have a houseful of children? You'd be such a good dad."

The car ate up another two miles before he answered. "It just never felt right," he said.

"It's not too late," she said.

His head turned sharply. "What do you mean?"

"It's not too late. You can still find someone wonderful to spend your life with, to have your children."

He sighed. "Yeah, I'll start working on that."

They didn't talk again until he pulled into the driveway of the old house. Lights were on, both upstairs and downstairs, making it look welcoming. Safe.

Adie should be the one who felt safe. That was her job as a mother, to make her daughter feel safe. To be safe.

And she had failed.

And her son, who made her feel inadequate on her best days, was in the house. She would see the disgust in his eyes.

Bray opened his door. Got out. Walked around the car and opened her door. She forced herself to move. To walk up the steps, across the front porch, toward the door that she'd walked through a hundred times during high school when she and Bray had been dating.

When things had been simple. And she'd thought her life was going to be very different.

Bray opened the door, motioned for her to go in.

She did and was almost knocked over by the body that burst out of the kitchen.

Young, sweaty male. Gangling arms that hugged her until she couldn't breathe.

Keagan.

She pulled back. Held his thin face. "Oh, Keagan," she said.

"I love you, Mom," he said, his eyes only full of love.

It was exactly what she needed to keep going.

THE FIRST THING Bray noticed was that there was an extra person in the room that he hadn't expected.

Milo Hernandez. When Summer saw him, she hugged him.

"I called and told him about Adie," Trish said. "I told him he didn't need to come."

By the look on the man's face, it would take a bulldozer to move him out of the house. And the look he was giving Bray said *go ahead and try*.

No way. This guy was solidly in Summer's and Trish's corners and that made him okay by him. And if Chase, a St. Louis police detective, was nervous about having an ex-con in the room, he wasn't showing it.

"Glad you're here," Bray said.

Milo gave him a short nod.

Then Bray focused on Nalana. She had her laptop open, waiting for them. There was a somewhat grainy picture of the two men entering the mall, two separate shots of them walking through the mall and then one final one of the man in the gray sweatshirt loitering near the spot where Summer had been attacked. The man who had been wearing the face mask had not yet pulled it on. He was midforties, and most interestingly, he had a port-wine stain on his cheek.

Nalana passed around her laptop. "Does anybody recognize either one of them?"

Summer studied the photos. She even let Keagan, who had literally begged to not have to leave the room, take a look. That was smart. It was possible that the boy had seen something that she hadn't.

But with the exception of Trish, who thought the man in the gray sweatshirt looked somewhat familiar but couldn't place him, nobody recognized either man.

"There are six separate driving entrances to this particular mall," Nalana added. "Cameras on all six. It took a while but we identified their car. A 2010 white Pontiac Grand Prix. We checked the plates. Unfortunately, they match up to a 2012 red Mustang that was totaled two months ago and currently residing in a junkyard."

"Did you talk to the junkyard?" Bray asked.

"Yeah. We tracked down the owner. Has no idea when the plates might have been lifted."

"Okay. What time did the Grand Prix arrive at the mall?" Bray asked.

Nalana gave Summer a quick glance. "About five minutes after Summer did."

He could see that the news hit Summer hard. That meant that she'd been followed from Ravesville, to the garage where Trish had picked up her car and then on to the mall.

"I guess I was pretty oblivious," said Summer, proving that he'd guessed her thoughts accurately.

"We both were," Trish said.

"You weren't any less observant than anybody else under the circumstances," Chase said. "When people have bad intent, it's hard to thwart their plans."

Summer looked up from the computer. "These are all shots of them entering the mall. What about when they left the mall?"

Nalana licked her lips. "It might be difficult for you…" Her voice trailed off.

"Show me," Summer said.

Nalana pressed a few keys. And there it was. The two men were walking in the parking lot. The man with the bulky jacket was carrying Adie. Her head was on his shoulder.

He could have been a dad carrying a sleeping child.

"Oh," Summer gasped. "They drugged her," she said.

Bray put a hand on her shoulder. "Probably. You recovered from that. She will, too."

"I'm going to kill them," she said, her back teeth jammed together.

"We will if we have to," Bray said easily. He pulled the computer screen away from her.

Milo looked satisfied with that answer.

"She's just a baby," Summer said. Then she looked up, saw her son, her mother, her sister. "No, she's not," she said more confidently. "She's a smart little girl. We've talked about what she should do if she was ever lost. She knows my cell-phone number, knows how to call me. She'll know that we're coming, that we'll find her."

Summer was being strong for her family. He wouldn't have expected anything else.

"What about video from the gas station?" Bray asked.

"My friend is working on that. It's a big chain. They have better web security than most. But he'll get it."

Bray pulled out the papers. Touching just the very edges, he spread them out on the table. "This is what was in…" He looked at Keagan. He'd been referring to Gary Blake as "Blake" or "the ex," but he didn't want Keagan to perceive that he was disrespectful of his dad and slip back into attitude. "…Officer Blake's safe-deposit box in St. Louis."

He looked at his brothers. "I suspect we all have had some experience in breaking codes. Probably you, too, Nalana."

"Limited," she said. "Most of it's done with computers now. I could probably ask for access to one, but I'm not sure that I can do it without somebody having to approve the request. It's out of my regular scope."

"I understand," Bray said. "I don't think that this is going to be that tough."

"We should start by identifying what's in common," Flora said.

Bray looked at Summer's mom, who was sitting on the edge of her chair, her eyes moving across the pages. She was right.

"Okay, what do we have?" he asked.

"Every page has just one line," Trish said, getting the dialogue going.

"Each line only has numbers, no letters," Cal added.

"Toward the end of each line," Summer said, "periods begin to be interspersed with the numbers. Every line has at least a couple periods. Some have more."

That was the easy stuff. It got harder from there. They studied the pages, sometimes walking around the table to get a better view.

"They range in length from thirty-nine digits to sixty-eight digits," added Chase.

More circling. No one said anything. Twenty minutes went by. Finally, Flora put a finger in the air. "Those six," she said, pointing, "have a common stretch of seventeen numbers."

Chapter Nine

That got everybody's attention. Flora pointed out the six and everyone studied them more carefully.

"We need a word with seventeen letters," Keagan said, his young voice high with emotion.

"Not necessarily," Bray said gently. "We can't assume that one number stands for one letter. For example, an *A* could be a 13. We'd be better off to think of groupings. What groupings or groups would Officer Blake have knowledge of?"

"How do we know this is Gary's list?" Flora asked. "Maybe it belongs to someone else and he was just keeping it for some reason."

"Maybe," Bray said. "We can't ignore possibilities, but I think it is more likely that if it was important enough for him to keep safe, then it's his list. Also, the paper matches the notebook on his desk. The notebook that was otherwise empty."

"Types of crimes," Raney said. "He's a cop. He would know people who committed the same type of crime."

"Good," Bray said. "What else?"

"Last names," Cal said. "Ravesville is a small town, and lots of people are related to one another. There could easily be six people with the same last name."

"Keep going," Bray said.

"Customer preferences," Cal said carefully. "You could have six who bought the same thing."

The adults around the table looked at one another, easily catching on that if Blake had been selling something, it was likely illegal. The comment went over Keagan's head. He didn't point out the fact that his dad wasn't in sales. Bray could see that Summer's eyes had turned thoughtful, as if she were remembering things and trying to piece them together with what Cal had suggested.

"What's the easiest way to create a code if you want to turn letters into numbers?" Bray asked.

"Easiest?" Chase considered. "Easiest is an *A* is a 1, a *B* is a 2 and so on."

"You got any blank paper?" Bray asked.

Cal opened a kitchen drawer and pulled out a spiral notebook. Bray flipped it open. Bray took the seventeen common letters and applied that logic and got gibberish.

"Or, to mix it up a little, *A* is a 5, *B* is a 10, *C* is

a 15 and so on. There could be a million combinations. We need a computer," Chase said.

"Three is his favorite number," Keagan said.

Bray tried assigning a 1 to an *A*, a 3 to a *B* and so on but got nothing. He wrote out the alphabet and next to the *A* put a 3. Then he put a 4 next to the *B* and so on. When he applied that logic, the room suddenly erupted with energy.

It was Ravesville. The seventeen digits stood for Ravesville.

Bray wanted to slap himself upside the head. He'd been too focused on the fact that it was one line and not in the traditional format of an address to give the idea due consideration.

From that point, it became easier. They hit a bump in the road and lost time when they realized that he'd used a different convention for the numbers versus letters. With numbers, he got tricky and used multiples of six. A six was really a 1, a twelve was really a 2 and so on. The periods in the line separated days, months and years.

392 Wolftail Road, Ravesville 3/3/2014 in code was 185412 25171482231114 201736 20324721241114147 18.18.120624.

"Ravesville. Hamerton. Port," Summer said, when they had finally deciphered all eleven. "All towns, relatively close. And the addresses, I don't know exactly where they are but I recognize some of the road names."

Everyone nodded. "You're right," Bray said. "I even recognize a few."

"And the dates. There's nothing older than two years ago," she added. She looked at Bray. "What the heck is this?"

Chase was busy mapping the locations on his iPad. "Some of these places don't look so great," he said. He showed them a picture of a run-down farmstead. Then a second one.

"Unfortunately, I think our only option is to go to these places and try to figure out what ties them together."

"Eleven places," Summer said. "While they are all in this general area, a couple of these points are probably at least one hundred miles apart. It's a big area to search. Especially in the dark."

It wasn't great circumstances, but he didn't see an alternative. "You want to wait until morning?" he asked.

"No," she said sharply. "Of course not."

"Relax," he said easily. "Me neither. But now I insist that you eat something. We can't be driving all over the countryside and have you pass out."

"Something quick," she said. She glanced at her watch.

He knew what it said. They'd worked as quickly as possible to break the code, but it was almost eleven o'clock.

"How about BLTs and fruit salad?" Raney said.

"That would be great," Summer said.

Raney and Nalana left the room. Trish gave her twin a hug, and she and Flora followed them.

"Keagan, you should probably try to get some sleep," Summer said. "We'll wake you if we hear anything."

"I shouldn't have told her that her dolls were stupid," Keagan said, his voice choked up.

Summer wrapped her arms around her son. "You are a really great older brother. Don't doubt that. How many times have you watched her for me lately? At least five times. I would never have allowed that if I didn't trust you a hundred percent. She adores you and she knows that you love her."

"Are we going to get her back?"

The question hung in the air. "Of course we are," Summer said, as if there could be no other conclusion. "I promise."

Bray was amazed. Summer was fearful down to the marrow of her bones, yet there was no way she was going to let her son know that. Now was the time for reassurance, for hope.

He was going to do everything in his power to make sure that this woman didn't have to go back on her promise. "Keagan, you can take my room upstairs. First door. Bathroom across the hall."

Once the boy was upstairs with the door closed,

Summer put her head in her hands. "I hope I didn't just make a very bad mistake," she said softly.

Bray wrapped an arm around her, aware that his brothers and Milo were watching. "You did exactly right," he said. "Exactly right."

He looked at Chase. "You and Raney are okay with staying here with Trish, Keagan and Flora?"

"Absolutely," Chase said.

"I'll stay with them," Milo said. "Then you and Raney can search, too. I could probably get us some additional resources fairly quickly, too, if we need them."

Bray didn't even want to contemplate who those resources might be. But Milo standing guard made sense. Summer and Trish trusted him implicitly. They were good judges of character. But how would Chase feel about leaving Milo in the house without any Hollisters present?

"Do you have a gun?" Chase asked.

As an ex-con, he should not. Milo lifted up his loose shirt. He was carrying a 9 mm. "I'm a good shot and won't hesitate when it comes to protecting them."

"Good enough for me," Chase said. Bray let out his breath. Emergencies made strange bedfellows.

"Okay, we'll split into three groups. Chase and Raney, Cal and Nalana, and Summer with me. Chase and Cal, you can each take three. They're the ones farthest out, so you'll have the most travel time. Summer and I'll take the remaining five. We ought to be able to cover everything within a couple hours. And…and maybe we'll get lucky. We might only have to look at two or three."

"It's a plan," Cal said.

"Okay. Be careful," Bray added, knowing it was unnecessary. Cal was a former navy SEAL and Nalana was an FBI agent. Chase was an experienced detective and, well, quite frankly, he wasn't going to let anything happen to Raney. They could certainly handle themselves. But he also knew that good cops, the very best ones even, could let their emotions get in the way when the safety of a child was at stake.

And mothers? Well, it went without saying that Summer should not be looking for her own child. Objectivity had gone out the virtual window the minute that thug had pushed her at the mall.

But he also knew that he didn't have the heart to ask her to wait at home. It meant that he'd need to be super vigilant and smart enough to protect both of them.

It wouldn't help anyone if Adie was found safe and sound but lost her mother in the process. And the idea of that possibility hit him like a .38 in the gut.

"What's wrong?" Cal asked.

"Nothing," Bray said, waving his hand. He

needed to get his head straight. Fast. "Can I use this?" he asked, picking up Chase's iPad.

"Sure," Chase said. He looked at Cal and inclined his head toward the kitchen. Both men walked out, leaving him alone with Summer.

"Your family is pretty great," she said.

"Your mom was the one who cracked the code open. Her recognizing that there were common stretches of numbers really helped."

"Sudoku and crosswords pay off," she said. She closed her eyes.

He started plugging in addresses.

"What are you doing?" Summer asked after a few minutes.

"A reverse lookup on the address." He kept going, finally pushing a list in Summer's direction. "Recognize any of these names?"

"This guy eats at the restaurant," she said.

Richard Bridge. He shuffled through the stack of pages one more time, stopping at the eighth page. "His address is 4903 Brewster Road."

She shook her head. "Richard Bridge has to be at least eighty-five years old. He lives in the assisted-living facility on the edge of town. He might have lived on Brewster Road at one time." She studied the names again. "Why are there only seven names? There are eleven addresses."

"The other four don't come up with anything. Not sure what that means."

Raney poked her head into the dining room. "Food's ready," she said.

BRAY MOTIONED FOR her to precede him out of the room. Then he caught up and pulled her chair out for her. Did the same for her mother, who was moving toward the table. Would have probably assisted Trish but Cal beat him to it.

The Hollister men had old-fashioned manners. Polite. Protective. Brave. White knights in shining armor.

Bray with his too-long hair and dangerous eyes would laugh at the comparison.

While they were eating, Bray continued to study the iPad and make notes in the spiral notebook. Finally, he looked up. "This probably isn't quite right," he said, "and certainly not to scale, but I wanted to get a feel for the relationship of one location to the next."

There was a big X with eleven smaller Xs around it. "I assume the big X is Ravesville," she said.

He nodded.

She pointed at one of the closer ones. "How far is this from Ravesville?"

He bent his thumb at the first joint. "This represents thirty miles."

It was a crude map, but it did the trick. She pointed at the two Xs the farthest from the big X.

"I underestimated. It means that between these two points, there's almost two hundred miles."

"That's why we're dividing and conquering."

She sucked in a deep breath. His ability to systematically work the clues probably served him well as a DEA agent.

The BLT was delicious, but she could force herself to eat only half along with a couple of bites of fruit. Halfway through the quick meal, Nalana's cell phone beeped.

She picked it up. "We have something on the gas receipt." She went to get her computer that she'd left in the dining room. Within seconds, she was pulling up a video image of the white Grand Prix pulling into the station. The man in the gray sweatshirt got out of the passenger side and began to pump the gas. His hood was up. When he finished, he motioned for the driver of the car, who was not clearly visible, to move forward. Then a pale green Maxima pulled in and he put gas in that vehicle, too. Then he pulled cash from his pocket and walked into the convenience store, presumably to pay.

He'd pumped forty-two gallons because he'd filled two cars. Now the receipt made sense. But who was the guy in the green car? The angle of the camera was all wrong to see the drivers of the vehicles; it was positioned to see the pump and the person standing next to it. There was one other angle that picked up the license plate.

They already knew the license plate for the Grand Prix was not good. The green car didn't even have one.

"The party is getting bigger," Bray said, running his tongue over his teeth.

Nobody answered. The man in the green car was just one more person to worry about. She pushed her plate aside. Bray frowned at her, but he didn't ask her to eat more. Instead, he carried both their plates to the sink and pulled his car keys from his pocket. "We'll stay in touch," he told the group.

Trish stood up and hugged Bray first. "Take care of her," she said.

Then she hugged Summer. "You are stronger than you think."

It was similar to what Summer had told Trish when Rafe had unexpectedly died.

Sometimes life was just so damn hard.

They were back in the car before she spoke. "Chase and Raney are supposed to get married on Saturday."

"I don't think they're worried about that right now," he said.

"They should be," she said bitterly. "None of us should have to be worrying about something like this."

Bray shrugged. "No argument on that. But that's not going to be our focus. We've made a lot of progress in a few hours. Finding the safe-deposit key in those boots was very important."

"We don't know that for sure. These addresses may mean nothing."

He plugged the first address into his GPS. She looked at the estimated travel time. Thirty-nine minutes. It would be after midnight when they arrived.

Way past bedtime for a five-year-old. She prayed that Adie was somewhere where she could actually sleep.

Bray was looking at her, his eyes gentle with concern. "They mean something. Not sure what, but something. And I have to believe that's getting us one step closer to Adie."

She blinked back tears. "How can you be so sure? So positive?"

He reached for her hand and cradled it between his own. His skin was warm, a little rough. Wonderful. "I know what you're doing," he said. "You're trying to prepare yourself for more disappointment. But it's okay to be hopeful. It's okay to expect the best."

"Is that how you do your job every day, Bray? Is that how you live in a world of drug dealers and all the bad people associated with that business?"

"It doesn't hurt to be able to see the positive,"

he said. Then he looked at their joined hands. "I wasn't able to always do that," he said.

"What do you mean?"

"When I came back from the Marines and you'd married Gary, I didn't think I'd ever be positive about anything again. I thought my life was over."

She could feel her throat threaten to close. "I'm sorry, Bray. I really am."

He looked as if he wanted to ask for more of an explanation, but then he shook his head sharply. "We should go."

He was giving her a pass. If she had any guts, she'd tell him the truth.

"You're right," she said, buckling her seat belt. She turned up the radio.

Chapter Ten

Wednesday, 11:30 p.m.

Now that they were back on the road, Summer was quiet. It gave him a moment to think.

The abductors had initially told Summer that they had a question about her ex-husband. But they hadn't asked her the question. They'd simply knocked her out and taken Adie.

What was the likelihood that the men didn't have something to do with Gary's disappearance?

Almost none.

And the only reason that they would need his child was if they meant to somehow use the child to force Blake to talk or to do something he wasn't inclined to do.

It was a powerful bargaining chip. And one that would force most men to act quickly.

Unless the guy was a real ass.

He wished he knew more about Blake and

what made him tick. And how much he cared for his daughter.

But those weren't the kind of questions that he could ask Summer. She was smart. In a minute, she'd understand the path his brain was taking. He wasn't going to plant a seed that Blake might sacrifice his own child to save himself.

Fifteen minutes away from their destination, his GPS took them off the highway and onto a secondary paved road. But ten minutes later, after two more turns, pavement ended and it turned into rough gravel. He had to reduce his speed to forty-five, and even so, rocks were bouncing up and hitting the vehicle.

On both sides of the road were open fields. The fall harvest had happened at least a month ago and now it was just acres of chopped-off stalks and clods of dirt. It was a clear night, but there was only a quarter moon. Visibility was adequate for fifteen or twenty yards but faded fast.

At least it wasn't raining or snowing.

He almost smiled. He'd heard the story about how Cal had found Nalana in a snowdrift during a freak early-winter storm. She'd had bad guys on her tail.

They'd survived that. He and Summer would survive this.

And they would rescue Adie. No other option was acceptable.

"You have arrived at your destination on the right."

The woman on his GPS sounded pretty confident, but Bray wasn't all that sure. There was a mailbox that somebody had knocked over, lying in the grass at the edge of the overgrown lane. He pulled off to the side of the road and killed his lights.

"We walk in from here," he said.

"I wish I'd worn jeans," Summer said.

She had on a red sweater, a black-and-white skirt that was just short enough to be interesting and black tights. Her shoes were black flats. She had on a blue-jean jacket with a scarf around her neck. It was what she'd worn to the mall. He probably should have told her to change into jeans, but he hadn't been thinking about clothing.

"I hope there aren't any snakes," she added.

He really hoped he found a couple of the two-legged variety.

He handed her a flashlight and grabbed the other one for himself. He carried it in his left hand. Using his right hand, he opened the middle console and removed his gun. He tucked a couple of extra clips into his vest pocket. They jostled against the lock-picking set that Chase had tossed him just before they'd left the house.

They quietly shut their car doors and started up the lane. It had deep ruts and Bray could see faint vehicle tracks. It was impossible to know how recently they'd been made. "Keep your light down," he said. "Don't wave it around."

The lane was a good quarter mile in length. And there was no pot of gold at the end of it. Nope. Just a dilapidated old two-story white farmhouse with a crumbling foundation on the north side that gave it an overall slightly lopsided look. Behind it were two outbuildings. One was a midsize barn, missing most of one side. The second was much smaller, maybe the size of a two-car garage. It was in better shape.

There wasn't a light on in the entire property and it had a deserted feel. But that did not mean that Adie couldn't be somewhere. People had been known to take children and stash them in isolated places.

This place meant something to Gary Blake. Meant enough that he'd rented a safe-deposit box to preserve the record.

"Are we going inside?" Summer whispered.

"Yes," he said. "Doing okay?"

He heard her breathing and saw her square her shoulders. "Don't worry about me," she said.

Yeah, like that was going to happen. "Let's go. Stay behind me."

He waited until she nodded. Then he started forward. There was no sidewalk, so he went through the yard. There were dry weeds up to his knees and patches of black dirt. No grass. He stopped twice to listen. Didn't hear anything.

He motioned for Summer to stand on one side of the door and he took the other. Then he reached for the doorknob.

Locked.

That didn't necessarily mean that nobody was inside. Even if the house was abandoned, any number of people in the backwoods of Missouri might be attracted to it. And most of them up to no good. None of them would welcome a visit.

He rapped loudly on the door.

Waited.

A second time.

He pulled out his tools and within minutes had the door open. He kicked it with the toe of his boot. Then he stepped forward, gun drawn.

It was pitch-black.

He listened. Waited for a sound that would tell him that somebody lurked in the dark corners.

But it was quiet. He used his flashlight. The house was empty, with the exception of two folding chairs that were in what was once probably the living room.

He turned and motioned for Summer to come in.

There was threadbare carpeting and an over-whelmingly bad smell of cat urine. There were no draperies, just old white ill-fitting shades on all the windows. He flipped his flashlight up. There were electrical connections for ceiling lights but no bulbs.

"I'm going upstairs," he whispered.

It looked about the same as the downstairs. The three bedrooms were empty, and when he poked his head in the bathroom, he saw that there was no water in the toilet. He tried the faucet. Nothing.

He went back downstairs and almost had a heart attack when he didn't see Summer. Then he heard her in the back of the house. She was stand-ing in the kitchen. Most of the cupboard doors had been removed. The shelves were bare. There was an old stove but no other appliances.

He saw a door that likely led to the basement. He motioned to Summer that he was going to look.

It was a stone basement that smelled damp. There was a furnace and water heater, both of which looked as if they hadn't worked in several years.

There was no five-year-old child.

He went back upstairs. "There's nobody here," he said in a normal tone.

"Now," Summer said.

"What do you mean?"

"The folding chairs aren't dusty. Somebody has sat in them recently."

She'd have made a hell of a cop. "I know. But it might have been last week," he added. They didn't want to add two plus two and come up with five. There was no reason to think that this house had anything to do with Adie's disappearance.

Other than the fact that it was on a list that had been in Blake's safe-deposit box.

"I'm fairly confident that whoever lived here had a cat," she said drily.

"That smell does linger. Maybe that's why the owners left—they couldn't stand it any longer." He moved to the door. "I'm going to check the other two buildings."

"I don't think she's here," she replied.

"I don't, either," he said. "But we need to look, just in case."

Adie wasn't in either of the other buildings. They were both empty, although there was a pile of leaves in one corner of the smaller building that made it look as if someone might have left the door open and the wind had blown them in.

He crumpled one of the leaves in his hand. It was still moist. From this fall for sure. So at one point in the recent past, the open door had been closed. By somebody.

Probably the person who had dusted off the folding chairs with their back end.

He had a pretty good idea of what the place was.

And there were two options. Blake had been a cop. He might have been investigating something that led him to this address.

Although this was clearly out of the jurisdiction of the Ravesville Police Department.

They walked back through the door and he pulled it shut behind them. "Summer, what's the drug situation around here? Did your ex ever get involved in any investigations?"

"Rural Missouri probably isn't all that different from other rural areas. Of course there are drugs. Just like there are drugs in cities. You know about that."

"I do. But the distribution method is different in the city versus a more rural area. Isolation offers opportunity that a city of eight million doesn't have. Plus, in the city, we quite frankly have more resources than the rural area."

"Nobody has been making meth in that house. Unless meth smells like cat urine."

He shook his head. "Not making it here. But maybe it's a drop-off point. No need to have a recliner—a folding chair will do. Customers are in and out. Nobody lingers. I'd really like to know if your ex had a legitimate reason to know about this place."

She blinked several times. He could tell she was thinking. Processing. Finally, she shook her head. "Lately, Gary has been so volatile. The least little thing set him off. And I know that can be a sign of drug use. But I don't think he was. I really don't. Why does it have to be drugs? Why couldn't it be something else?"

"It could be, and I'll admit to having a predisposition to thinking drugs first. But I've got to tell you, it feels right.'"

"We just don't know what side Gary was on," she said.

Speaking of sides, he recalled that his brothers had told him that Gary had been involved with Sheila Stanton, who had recently left town unexpectedly. "Do you know anything about his relationship with Sheila Stanton?"

"He *had* a relationship with Sheila?"

He hated to be the one to tell her this. "According to Chase and Raney. They thought that might have clouded his judgment."

"Maybe. The Stantons were old money in Ravesville. But I never thought a whole lot of her. She treated people like dirt. I remember when Chase dated her," she said. "He was maybe a year or two out of high school. I was always surprised when I saw them together."

"Raney is ten times the woman," Bray said.

"For sure. When we first met, Chase was pretending that they were already married. We later learned that he was protecting her because she was a witness at an upcoming trial. It's nice to know that they're going to make their cover story a reality."

"And assuming that Sheila didn't leave town unexpectedly because she was torn up over Chase, we should probably figure out where she went. Do you have anybody that you can ask?"

"One of my good customers did her hair. She might know."

"When we get to the car, call her," he said.

"She'll be sleeping."

She was right. It wasn't the kind of question that you got somebody out of bed for. Certainly not under usual circumstances, and they didn't want anybody thinking there was anything unusual going on. "Okay. We'll wait a bit for that. Let's go to the next place on the list."

She turned to look at him. "Bray, I don't know what I'd be doing without you. I know I didn't have the right to ask you to help. But I knew that if anyone could find Adie, you could. Thank you for not sending me away."

She had tears in her eyes. And that was his undoing. He pulled her into his arms. And under a quarter moon, he kissed the woman who still held his heart in her hands. It was sweet and familiar, yet sharp and edgy and very different, too. She tasted of bacon and tomatoes, and it was easy to sink into her soft lips.

And he didn't stop until her body stiffened in response to the faraway sound of a barking dog. She pulled back. Her breath was coming fast. Her lips, wet from his, were trembling.

There were a thousand things he could say. A thousand questions he could ask. But now wasn't the time. "I would never send you away, Summer. Know that in your heart. Now let's get out of here."

SHE USED TO dream about kissing Bray Hollister again. When she was married, for sure. She'd hidden that from Gary, but in the end, he'd still known.

Even after the divorce, while the dreams had been less frequent, they'd been no less intense, no less of a painful reminder of all that she'd given up.

But now that it had actually happened, she realized that her dreams had paled in comparison. He'd left her as a boy and now he was a man. Big and strong and so very confident.

And he'd made her shake with need.

Somehow she'd managed to get herself back in the car, and now, as she hugged her door, she told herself that he was just a kind man comforting an old friend.

But as hard as she tried, she wasn't buying it.

He'd kissed her as if he'd been saving up for years. And she'd felt the energy all the way to her toes.

"How far is the next house?" she asked. Her daughter was missing. She was a horrible person to be thinking of anything else.

"Eighteen miles," he said.

His cell phone buzzed and he answered it. "Hey, Cal." Then he listened. Summer wished she could hear what Cal was saying. Whatever it was, Bray didn't look surprised. "Okay, go on to the next one," he said. He listened for another minute. Glanced at her. Gave her a soft smile. "She's fine," he said. "Strong." Then he hung up.

"You're giving me too much credit," she said.

He shook his head. "Cal just talked to Chase. They've each finished one search. Cal's property didn't even have a house, just an outbuilding. Nothing there. Chase found a rural farmhouse with no outbuildings. House still had some furniture but it was clear that nobody had been there for some time."

"So, in general, they found exactly what we did," she said.

He nodded. "Three down. Eight more to go."

She looked at the clock on the dashboard. "We're running out of time."

"We don't know that. They haven't called your cell phone yet."

"Maybe they're watching my house. Maybe they're wondering where I am. If I've gone to the police."

"They might be. But I don't think that can be helped. But that reminds me," he said. "Across the street from the café, there's a three-story building. Who lives on the second floor?"

"Why?"

"Today when we were leaving the restaurant, I saw somebody in the window, watching the café. When I came around the corner, he pulled back fast."

"He? That's odd. A single woman rents that space but she's always traveling. I've spoken to the owner of the building and she said that she's probably only seen her three or four times in the last year, but she doesn't care because the rent is always paid on time. Maybe she's letting someone stay there."

"Someone who didn't want to be seen."

"Or maybe someone who didn't want to seem nosy."

"Maybe. But it seemed to me that he was watching the café. And he didn't want me to know that."

Chapter Eleven

Her head was spinning. In addition to the mysterious list and the news about Sheila Stanton and Gary, now a suspicious watcher merited consideration. Was that somehow also related to Gary and this mess? It was really just too much to process.

And it had been seven and a half hours since they'd taken Adie. A lifetime to a child. A horribly long time to be frightened or hurt.

She felt the BLT in her stomach rumble. She pressed her hands to her midsection.

"What's wrong?" Bray asked.

The man saw everything. Thought of everything. He'd been that way when he was young, too. That was why when he'd come home from the Marines, she'd barely given him any explanation. She'd known that he'd see through her lies if given half a chance.

"Nothing different," she said, hoping he'd let it go.

He gave her a long look but didn't press it. He punched the address for the next location into the GPS and they took off. "Has Gary dated anyone else besides Sheila since your divorce?"

It was a logical question. He was methodically thinking of all possible leads. Still, it was awkward talking about Gary to Bray. "A couple of times that the kids were there, Maggie Reynolds joined them for dinner. She worked at the library. I think Keagan understood that his dad was dating but Adie didn't get it. I don't think it worked out because they haven't mentioned seeing Maggie for at least six months. Plus, I've seen Maggie with Porter Gates several times. He owns the gas station at the edge of town. The one you used to work at."

"I know Porter. We both started at the station on the same day. Odd to think that could be me."

"What?" she asked.

"When I got back to Ravesville, if things had been different, maybe I'd have gotten my old job back at the station. In time, maybe I'd have decided to buy it."

She couldn't see Bray doing that. She'd always known that he was destined for bigger and better things than Ravesville. And even at eighteen, she'd worried that she was holding him back because she'd known that she couldn't leave her mom. Maybe it was another reason why she'd ultimately agreed to The Plan. That was what she'd coined what Gary, her mother and she had come up with that long-ago night. The Plan.

It made it seem less half-baked, less crazy. Less wrong.

They rode in silence for another five minutes. Then Bray turned to look at her. "If it's not a jilted lover from Gary's past who might want to do him harm, is there anybody that you might have been seeing who would still consider him competition?"

She could feel heat in her face and was grateful that the car was dark with the exception of the dimly lit dashboard. Could she be as blunt with him as she'd been with Trish? Why not? "I'm divorced with two kids, a mortgage and a business loan. I'm not a great catch."

"You're kidding, right?" he said, his tone incredulous.

She felt very warm. There wasn't a woman alive who wouldn't want Bray Hollister to say something like that to them. But they were no longer seventeen-year-old kids flirting in a parked car. "I dated one person after the divorce," she said, carefully ignoring his remarks. "When Gary found out, he didn't react well. There were words. Anyway, my date ended up paying for dinner and for two tires that had been slashed. Of course, we couldn't prove it was Gary, but I think he quickly figured I wasn't worth the trouble."

"I guess I hope your ex is still okay, but I've got to tell you, he's tough to like."

"I know. More so the last couple years. In fact, now that you mention it, he's been having trouble with another officer on the Ravesville police force."

"What kind of trouble?"

"I don't know. We were divorced by the time Daniel Stone started, but I heard a few things at the restaurant that he wasn't getting along with Gary. I think the chief had to get involved on a couple of occasions."

"So that might be someone else to look at," Bray said.

"Our list is growing," she said. "We should be eliminating possibilities, not adding."

"Better this than not having anything to go on," Bray said.

True. At least she was doing something. Otherwise, she'd simply be staring at a silent phone.

Their GPS led them to a graveyard. "Are you sure this is it?" Summer asked. She did not like graveyards. Once every year, she made herself visit the one where her father had been buried for the past seventeen years but she always disliked it. She rolled down her window so that she could better see the address that had been painted on the gate.

Don't walk across my grave.

She swore she could hear the warning in the soft night wind. It was a small graveyard, like one you'd see in most any rural community. Maybe a couple hundred graves, a few with big headstones, many with much smaller and modest markings. There was a rusty iron fence around the perimeter with a big gate, wide enough for a hearse.

Bray pointed at the address. "Matches what we have," he said.

"I was afraid of that." She opened her door, her flashlight gripped tightly in her hand. Bray joined her. The gate was not locked, swinging open easily when Bray flipped the wide latch.

"I saw a movie once," she whispered. "A man had kidnapped a child and he buried her alive in an old grave. There was a pipe sticking up from the ground. That was how she got her air. It was horrible."

"It was a movie," he said gently. "But we'll keep our eyes open."

There were three large trees in the cemetery but they had lost all their leaves. Now they looked like hulking giants with thousands of gnarled and knotted arms. There was one tall light, in the very middle, which meant that very little light reached the far edges.

"You start at that side. I'll take this one," Bray said. "Be careful and don't trip."

She saw that there were many headstones that were flat into the ground. She glanced at the dates. Many dated back to the late nineteenth century. There was one, a woman who'd been born in 1889 and died in 1918, a short twenty-nine years later. *Alice Whay, wife of Jonas and mother of Thadias.* She found herself saying a silent prayer. *Please, Alice. I'm so sorry you were taken too soon from your own child, but please, please, if Adie is here, watch over her. Please do not let her be alone.*

And because her emotions were a damn roller coaster, the next minute she was kicking at some dirt, mad as hell that it was highly likely that drug dealers had seen fit to denigrate this space by using it as a distribution point.

She saw Bray stop near a freshly dug grave and her heart plummeted. She could not move. "Bray?" she said, her voice carrying in the night.

He waved. "It's okay," he said. "It's a new grave but not that new. The gravestone says the man died in September."

She sucked in a deep breath and kept walking. They met in the middle. "I'm going to check that shed." Bray spoke softly.

The white shed with peeling paint was at the rear of the graveyard. It was not any bigger than most people's family rooms. It had two small windows and it was dark inside. She followed him.

There was a padlock on the door. "What are you going to do?" she asked.

"I'm not leaving here until I know she's not in there," Bray said simply. He took his flashlight and knocked out one of the windows.

Then he stuck his upper body inside, along with his flashlight. After a long moment, he pulled back. "It's storage. Lawn mower and shovels and rope. Things like that. She's not inside."

They went back to the car. "How many times?" she asked.

"How many times what?"

"How many dates are next to this address?"

Bray picked up the list. "Four."

"I hate them for that," she said simply.

"Me, too," he said and reached to plug in the next address.

Twenty-five minutes later, they arrived in the neighboring community of Port. It was even smaller than Ravesville, with a population of 753. Or so the sign at the edge of town said.

The GPS led them to a four-story building at the intersection of Main Street and Lincoln, the only cross street in the two-block business district. Roosevelt Elementary. "I didn't think it could get worse than a graveyard," she said. "Schools should be sacred."

"If it makes you feel any better, it looks as if this one has been closed for a couple years."

"Not much better," she said. "But I think you're right. This school district was consolidated into Ravesville about two or three years ago. That's happening all over the country. There are probably empty schools in lots of small towns."

"In big towns, too. But in my world, most of the drugs are distributed at functioning schools, mostly by the low-level echelon. The truth is, we could bust somebody every day. Multiple people every day. Sometimes we have to just let it happen because we're ultimately trying to get the small creep to lead us to a bigger creep."

"That must drive you crazy," she said.

"Yep," he said.

She could tell he didn't want to talk about it. He was the type who wouldn't want to turn his back on any wrongdoing.

"How many dates for this one?" she asked.

He looked. "Three. But the last one was just three weeks ago. I think that was the most recent one of all."

There were several open spots in front of the school and she expected him to pull into one of them. She was surprised when he didn't.

"Listen," he said, "I'm going around the block a couple times." He turned on Lincoln Avenue. It had simple single-family homes on both sides with detached garages. Middle class. Maybe not even that. He made a couple more turns and was back on Main Street. All the businesses on the street were closed. There was a community center for seniors, an alterations shop, a thrift store and a cash store. There was a small grassy area between the cash store and the school.

It was depressing.

The small community was asleep. Bray parked. He didn't get out of the car.

"What's wrong?" she said.

"I don't know. Something just doesn't feel right. See that gas station?" he said, pointing up the street.

"Yeah."

"It's got an open sign blinking in the window but everything else is dark."

"So, some clerk forgot to shut it off when he or she left for the night."

"Maybe," he said. He still didn't move.

Tingling started at the base of her spine and moved upward. "Bray, do you think she's here? Is that it?"

He turned to her. "I'm sorry. It's not that. It's different. Let's go check it out. Just stay close, okay."

"How are we going to get in?"

"Well, it would have been easy if they hadn't boarded up those windows."

It was one of those buildings where the first-floor windows were level with the ground.

"Let's go around back and I'll boost you up. If you stand on my shoulders, you should be able to reach the windows on the second level. If you can get in, then you can come open the door for me. I'd rather not have to break it if I don't have to."

"What if there is an alarm?"

"Then we're going to run like hell," he said. "This is an unincorporated village. They don't have their own police. Probably state cops would need to respond."

He opened his door. There was enough street light that they didn't need their flashlights. They hurried around the school, staying close to the building. "Let's go," Bray said, bending down. "Get on my shoulders."

She froze. It was exactly what he'd told her in the car but she hadn't really processed it. He wanted her to sit on his shoulders. Then he was going to stand, and then so was she. Simple enough. She'd have the sides of the building to balance against. She wouldn't fall.

But she was going to have to wrap her legs around him and plaster herself up against the back of his neck.

Now the tingling was in other parts besides her spine.

"Uh…I've got a skirt on."

"I'm not going to be looking up it," he said, his tone gently exasperated. "And…it's not as if I haven't seen it before."

If that was supposed to make her feel better, it was having the opposite effect. It had been more than fifteen years since she and Bray had been lovers, but her body remembered.

"Come on," he said, looking up at her. He patted his shoulders. "I won't drop you."

She could do this. She could. She hiked her skirt up and put her left leg over his left shoulder. Did the same with her right leg. Her thighs were wrapped around his neck. She scooted up so that her bottom wasn't hanging in the air.

Yup. The tingling parts liked it.

He put his strong hands around her calves. She could feel the heat through her thick tights. He stood up. "Careful," he whispered.

The time for that was long past.

"Okay, now you stand up," he said.

She pulled her left leg up, got her foot situated on his shoulder. Did the same with her right foot. Thankful for her flat shoes and strong thigh muscles, she started to rise. When she was fully upright, she could easily see in the window. It was dark inside. She turned on her flashlight. "I can see some—"

"You two just step away from the building. Keep your hands where I can see them. I've got a gun and I know how to use it."

Chapter Twelve

Gun! She teetered on his shoulders. Bray's hands tightened on her calves. "We'll be happy to do that," he said, his voice calm. "I don't want to drop her. I'm going to turn around and squat down so that she can jump off. Okay?"

He clearly didn't want to make any unexpected moves. She wanted to twist around, to see who was behind them, but she followed Bray's lead. It couldn't be a cop. No police officer would say that he had a gun and knew how to use it.

"Okay, but don't try anything funny."

It was another line from a bad movie. Bray did exactly what he'd told the man he was going to do. He turned, carefully squatted so that she could dismount and then promptly pushed her behind him.

But not before she had seen that the older man, in a red-and-black plaid jacket and a black stocking cap, did indeed have a gun. A rifle. Pointed at them.

"I told Mary that you'd be back. Your kind always are." The man's voice was scratchy, as if he had a cold.

"Sir, I'd appreciate it if you'd lower your gun," Bray said, his voice still calm.

It dawned on her that this was unlikely the first time that he'd faced a gun.

But those other times he hadn't had her to worry about. She suspected her presence there was weighing heavily on Bray. He was that kind of guy. She stood very still, not wanting to distract him.

"You going to leave some more of your poison? You going to ruin another young man's life? Ruin his family?"

The man's voice had cracked at the end and she had a pretty good idea of what they were facing. Either this man's son or grandson or someone special to him had been harmed, maybe killed, by drugs that had been delivered here. She felt ill with the thought that Gary might have had something to do with it.

"My name is Brayden Hollister," Bray said. "I am a federal agent with the Drug Enforcement Agency. I know about the trouble here, sir. I've come to help."

There was a long pause. She couldn't stand it.

She looked around Bray. The man was staring at them, his mouth open. He still had not lowered his gun.

"I'd be happy to show you some identification if you'll put your gun down," Bray said.

The man shook his head. "We can't get no police to pay attention. Why the hell is a federal agent suddenly taking notice?"

"The activity here, sir, is part of a larger operation. The wrongdoing will not go unpunished. How about if I reach into my pocket and pull out my identification? I'll toss it over to you."

The man must have nodded. She wondered briefly if Bray was going to go for his gun but he didn't. He did exactly what he'd said. He reached into his pocket and pulled his billfold out. Then he tossed it toward the man.

She peeked again. The man picked it up and flipped it open. He studied the badge or whatever it was that Bray carried with him.

The man's shoulders started to shake and his gun wobbled dangerously.

"Put your gun down," Bray ordered, his voice sharp.

"Who's she?" the man asked.

"None of your concern," Bray answered. "I'm going to ask you one more time—put your gun down."

The man knelt down and laid his rifle on the

ground. Bray moved fast, grabbing it and handing it to her. Then he pulled his own gun, looking around. "Is there anyone with you?" he asked.

The man shook his head. "My brother and I've been taking turns for two weeks, watching the building. He owns the gas station up the road. It was my night."

"What happened here?" she asked.

"My Bobby had been turning his life around. Making something of himself. Providing for his wife and his child. And then his wife asked for a divorce. Sent him back into a bad time. If I'd have known that he was doing drugs again, I'd have tried to stop him."

There was more to the story. She could feel it. Had the drugs killed him? "Where is Bobby now?" she asked.

"Flat on his back at the rehabilitation hospital. He isn't ever going to walk again. He took those damn drugs and thought he could go a hundred miles an hour on the highway."

She didn't ask for the details. She'd heard enough. "I'm sorry," she said. "For your son. For your family."

The man said nothing.

"Do you know who sold your son the drugs?" Bray asked.

The man shook his head. "I don't want to know them. I just want them to pay."

"What's your name, sir?" Bray asked.

"Walt Meeker."

"And is Mary your wife?"

"Yes."

"Okay, Walt. You go home and tell Mary that the people who sold those drugs to your son are going to be punished. I'm going to give you back your gun, but I need you to promise to put it away and let law enforcement do their jobs."

Bray nodded at Summer and she stepped forward to hand Walt his gun. He took it without a word. He stared at them for a long minute. Then he turned and slowly started walking down the street. A block away, he got into a pickup truck. They heard it start, and when he pulled out, he turned off before he passed them.

Summer let out the breath she'd been holding. "That was brilliant. To admit to being a DEA agent. It was the one thing you could have told him that would have made him put his gun down."

"Let's get out of here," Bray said, clearly uncomfortable with the praise.

"What about looking inside?"

"There's no need. Adie isn't here. Walt and his brother have been watching this building for days. They'd have seen activity."

He was right. She walked back toward the car. "I can't help feeling bad that we lied to him. He thinks there is going to be some justice for his injured son."

"I didn't lie," Bray said. "Right now, we have to focus on finding Adie. But once we do that, I can focus on helping Walt even the score."

They got in the car. "Do you think he would have shot us?" she asked.

Bray didn't answer for a long minute. When he did speak, his voice was hoarse with emotion. "I was a marine. Then a beat cop and now a federal agent. I have faced my share of danger. And I have never been as scared as I just was when I thought that old man might accidentally get a shot off and I'd have lost you. Again."

His words burned her. "Oh, Brayden," she said.

She was suddenly across the console and in his arms. Their kiss was hot and greedy and full of all the emotion of potential loss and exhilarating gain.

He put his hand under her shirt, cupped her breast, stroked the tip of her nipple. His tongue was in her mouth. Blinding need streaked through her.

She wanted. She desperately wanted.

And then she heard a phone ring. Thought it was hers at first. She pulled back, yanking her shirt down. Heat rose to the top of her head.

Bray was answering his phone. "Yeah, Cal," he said.

The guilt swamped her. Her daughter was missing. Missing. And she'd been sprawled over Bray like a teenager in heat.

He ended the call. But he didn't look at her. He just stared out the windshield.

"What did he say?" she asked.

"No luck. He and Nalana are on their way to look at the last address on their list."

"Six down, five to go," she said. She was not going to talk about the kiss.

"About what just happened," he said, his voice sounding strained.

"No," she said. "We are not going to talk about it. We are not going to think about it. And we sure as hell aren't going to do it again."

He drummed his fingers on the steering wheel. Emotion poured off of him, almost in visible waves. He turned to her. "Fine. But when this is over, we damn sure are going to talk about it. I let you push me away fifteen years ago, Summer. I slunk away like a whipped dog. And that was the biggest mistake I ever made. I should have fought for you. I'm not going to make that same mistake again, even if it means that I have to fight *with* you."

She wasn't sure what to think about that. But whatever the reprieve, she was grateful for it. Adie. She needed to think about Adie. "Now what?" she said.

"We go to the next address." He punched it into his GPS and stared at the screen. "We know this place," he said.

She looked. It was just outside of Ravesville. On the same road as Rock Pond. Based on the GPS, very close to Rock Pond.

She did not want to go there. Not with Bray. Not when her nerves were stretched to the point of breaking. But if Adie might be there, then nothing would keep her away.

"Let's go," she said.

It was a fifteen-minute drive. Bray turned down the road that led to the quarry and ultimately to Rock Pond.

"It's been years since I've been here," she admitted. After she'd married Gary, she'd come often, making up stories about going to the library or the grocery store so that she could come sit by the pond. Here was the one place that she had always felt closer to Bray. After Keagan had been born, she'd brought him with her, as if there were some way that she could introduce her young son to Bray. *Be happy for me*, she'd often thought. Always followed by *I'm so very sorry*.

She hadn't realized at the time that Gary knew, that he had seen her car there. She'd discovered that in one of their very ugly arguments that had happened shortly after she'd told him that she was leaving.

And after her divorce, when she was officially free of scrutiny, she hadn't been able to come anymore. It didn't feel right. She'd made a mess of things and she couldn't forgive herself, let alone seek forgiveness from Bray in a place that had been so special.

This was the first place they'd made love. They'd both been seventeen. It should have been awkward and hurried and uncomfortable. It had been sweet and slow and amazing.

"I was here on Tuesday night," he said.

She didn't know what to say to that. She settled on "Why?"

"Because after I left your house, I was really angry. I needed to calm down, to go someplace where I could think. There are good memories here."

She couldn't tell him how those memories had sustained her in the first few years of her marriage. "I didn't handle that conversation in my kitchen well. I always thought when the time came to have that discussion, I'd do a better job. That I would be able to be dispassionate."

"Dispassionate?" he repeated.

"Unemotional. Detached."

"I know what it means. I'm just surprised. That's the one thing you and I never had." He shook his head. "Dispassion."

He was right. Theirs had been an intensely passionate relationship. But they'd been so young. Really, just kids. What did they know about the real world, about all the things that would bury passion and make it easy to settle for safety?

"Looking for Adie out here in the dark will be like looking for a needle in a haystack," she said.

"I think it's not a likely hiding place," he said. "The only structure is the administrative offices for the quarry, but unless the kidnapper owns the quarry, I doubt that's the place."

"It's probably a really good spot to hand off drugs," she said. "Young people still come here. They drive around the pond, sometimes stopping. It would be as simple as one driver rolling down his window with the stuff and the driver in the other car handing over cash. How many dates on the sheet?"

He looked. "Five. The last one in May of this year."

"Maybe they avoid this spot during the summer months. Too much traffic, too many people hiding in the bushes."

"Getting poison oak on their…assets," he said, humor in his tone.

Who could forget that? "It was dark when I put the blanket down. We'd have been fine if we hadn't gone down to the pond afterward and wrapped ourselves up in that damn blanket." As it was, she'd been cradled in his lap, mostly protected. His bare back had taken the brunt of it.

"I itched for a damn week," he said. "But I couldn't exactly explain that to my mother, could I?"

Kids. They'd just been kids.

It wasn't supposed to last.

But it had hurt so much when it hadn't. "We should check the next place," she said.

He looked as if he wanted to say something else, but he nodded and started to enter the next address in his GPS. He stopped.

"What?" she said.

"I think it might be time to talk to the police."

"I thought you said that we were doing everything they could be doing?"

"Not for that reason. I want to talk to Daniel Stone. He's the cop who discovered that your ex was missing. Plus, there's known friction between him and your ex. I want to know more about that."

"He'll be in bed."

"I don't think so. Somebody has to work the night shift. I don't think Chief Poole is doing it."

"Are you crazy? I can't go to the police. They told me not to."

"We're not going to talk to him about Adie."

"But they won't know that. If someone is watching the police, all they'll see is me meeting with Stone. That will be enough for them to think the worst."

"That's why we need to think of another way," Bray said.

"I'm not at my creative best," Summer responded, sarcasm heavy in her tone.

"I've got an idea," he said. "You know my stepbrother, Lloyd Doogan?"

Summer nodded. "It's always hard for me to remember that he's actually related to you. I mean, I realize he's not blood, but your mother was married to his father. Earlier this fall, he showed up at a birthday party that was being hosted at the café for Gordy Fitzler. He was really drunk and I think Chase and Raney had to deal with him."

"I heard about that. Based on what Chase has told me, he seems to think Lloyd is trustworthy and not out to harm the Hollister family in any way."

"I'm not sure I see how Lloyd can help us. He's…he's slow," Summer said, as kindly as possible.

"I know. I don't know what the official diagnosis is, but I remember that he wasn't able to finish high school. His father used to say some cruel things about him. Mom used to say that Lloyd's drinking was his way of coping with a world that he didn't always understand. All I know is that I suspect it's not all that unusual for the Ravesville police to have to respond to some incident that Lloyd Doogan is involved in. If somebody is watching the police, they're not going to think anything of it. But when Daniel Stone responds, you and I are going to be there."

"It might work," she said.

"It better," he replied and pushed down on the accelerator. "Do you know Lloyd's address and phone?"

"No. I probably could figure out where he lives. Like I said before, there isn't that much rental property in Ravesville."

Bray tossed his cell phone at Summer. "That's okay. Text Chase and get the information from him."

She did, and within minutes, there was a return text. "He thinks Lloyd may have a phone but he doesn't have the number. He does have the address. It's just a few blocks away from the café."

"Let's hope he's home," Bray said.

"Do you think we should look at any more of these addresses?" Summer asked.

"Let's talk to Officer Stone first."

"I hope Lloyd Doogan is willing to assist," Summer said.

"Me, too," Bray said, gripping the steering wheel tighter. "If he's not, I'm not sure what we're going to do."

Chapter Thirteen

Thursday, 2:45 a.m.

Lloyd lived in a one-room apartment on the lower level of a three-story building. There was no doorbell, so Bray knocked. When there was no answer, he knocked a second time, harder.

A minute later, the door opened. Lloyd looked rumpled and disoriented but Bray didn't smell any alcohol. He was pretty confident that they'd simply awakened him.

"Hi, Lloyd," Summer said. "It's Summer Wright."

"Hello." He didn't ask why they were at his door. Maybe people showed up at his apartment at all hours of the day.

"Lloyd, I'm Bray Hollister. Do you remember me?"

Lloyd stared at Bray for a long minute. "Yes," he said finally.

Bray glanced over his shoulder at the dark

street, making sure they were still alone. "May we come in?"

Lloyd stepped back and they entered. The inside of the small apartment was dimly lit and smelled musty. There was a couch and one chair. There were three drying racks and all of them had wet clothes hanging over them. He suspected that Lloyd simply washed his clothes in the sink and that the expense of a Laundromat was money he didn't have.

Summer and Bray took the couch. Lloyd stood by the chair for a minute, then finally sat down.

Summer looked at Bray and he nodded. On the way here, they'd discussed the approach. Neither was sure what Lloyd would easily understand or be able to figure out. "I need your help," she said. "I need to talk to Officer Stone but I don't want anybody to know that I'm doing that. I want Officer Stone to come here so that I can talk to him."

Lloyd said nothing.

Bray leaned forward. "Lloyd, can you call the police department and tell them that you need an officer to come to your house?"

"I don't like the police," Lloyd said.

Of course he didn't. "They won't be upset once they know why you called them," he said. He hoped he was right. "All we need you to do is to call them and tell them that somebody broke into your apartment and you need the police to investigate."

Lloyd stared at them. "Did you break in?" he asked.

"No. No, we didn't, Lloyd," Bray said, trying hard to hang on to his patience. He was tired and frustrated, and he had no idea if this was worth their time. "But you're going to pretend that we did. And then when the police arrive, we will tell them the truth."

"Tomorrow is Thanksgiving," Lloyd said.

Summer nodded. "It is."

"Raney and Chase invited me to dinner," Lloyd said.

"That's nice," Bray said. "Summer and I'll be there, too."

"We're family," Lloyd said.

"Yes, we are," Bray said easily. "Do you have a phone, Lloyd?"

"In the kitchen." Lloyd got up and led them through the narrow doorway into a dark room. He turned on the light. The space was small but probably adequate for a single man. There was a stove, refrigerator and double sink. There was a small table with two chairs.

Lloyd had had frozen pizza for dinner. The box was still on the counter and his dirty plate was in the sink.

Most important, there was a green phone hanging on the wall. A good old-fashioned landline.

"Here's what you need to say," Bray said. "'My name is Lloyd Doogan and I live at 349 Plover Street in Ravesville and somebody broke into my apartment.'" Bray paused. "Can you repeat that for me, Lloyd?"

"My name is Lloyd Doogan. Somebody broke into my apartment. My address is 349 Plover Street in Ravesville."

"Close enough," Bray said. This might actually work. "The person who answers the phone might ask if the people who broke in are still there and you need to say no. Okay?"

Lloyd nodded.

Bray lifted the telephone receiver. He punched in 911 and handed the phone to Lloyd. He stood very close to Lloyd, attempting to hear the other end of the conversation so that he could prompt Lloyd appropriately.

Lloyd didn't need any prompting. He said his spiel just like he'd practiced.

"That was perfect, Lloyd," Bray said. "Thank you very much."

Lloyd didn't respond. He simply led them back to the living room, where he took the chair and they took their spots on the couch. They didn't talk. After a minute, Bray got up and brought both of the kitchen chairs into the living room.

Was it possible that they were putting their trust in the wrong man? What if this Daniel Stone was behind Gary's disappearance? It was no secret that they didn't get along. Was the relationship much worse than anyone else had suspected?

If he was behind Gary's disappearance, then it was a foregone conclusion that he had something to do with Adie's kidnapping.

Bray knew they were running out of time. Adie had been missing for ten-plus hours. And still no call. They had to take the risk of confronting Daniel Stone.

They heard a car pull up and then the slam of the door. Stone had arrived without lights or a siren. Probably didn't think Lloyd Doogan rated either.

There was a sharp knock at the door. Bray motioned for Lloyd to answer it.

"Lloyd?" Officer Stone had transferred from somewhere in the Deep South, and his accent hadn't faded in the time that he'd been in Ravesville. "You called 911 about a break-in?"

Lloyd nodded and stepped back. Officer Stone walked in. With his foot, Bray closed the door behind him. The officer swung around and started to reach for his gun.

Bray put his hands up. "I'm Bray Hollister. I think you know Summer Wright. We needed the opportunity to talk to you without anybody seeing us."

"Anyone else here?" Officer Stone asked.

"Nope."

"What's Lloyd got to do with this?"

"We asked him to make the call," Bray said. "My mother was married to his father."

"I guess I had heard that. You know, making a fake 911 call is a crime," Officer Stone said.

"I know. I'm a DEA agent in New York City. I'm hoping that you won't hold it against him once you hear our story. Can we sit?"

Officer Stone took one of the kitchen chairs, and Bray took the other. Summer sank down onto the couch and Lloyd took his chair. Bray looked at Summer, silently asking if she wanted to take the lead.

She drew in a deep breath. "I believe you know that, at one time, I was married to Gary Blake."

Daniel Stone nodded.

"We were divorced about two years ago. We have two children."

Another nod.

"This morning I learned that when Gary didn't show up for work as expected, you went to his house. There were signs of a fast departure and a small amount of blood at the scene."

Daniel didn't nod but he didn't look surprised. He wasn't giving anything away.

"I was questioned by Chief Poole but I did not have anything to do with it."

"I'm not sure where this is going," Officer Stone said.

"I want to know if you had something to do with it."

He let out something between a sigh and a laugh. "Summer, I can appreciate your concern for your ex-husband. But you need to leave the investigating to the police. If he's really missing, we'll find him."

If he's really missing.

He said it easily. Certainly not like a man who knew for sure what had happened to Gary. Summer glanced at Bray. He gave her a gentle nod.

"At five o'clock this afternoon, two men approached me at the Hamerton Mall. They said they wanted to ask me a question about my ex-husband. I was with my five-year-old daughter, Adie. They knocked me out with something and they took her."

The officer sat up straighter in his chair. "What's the demand?"

"There isn't one," Bray said.

Daniel Stone said nothing, but the look he gave Summer was sympathetic. "Where's your son?"

"With Trish."

"Are they alone?" Stone asked.

"Milo, our cook, is with them," Summer said.

"Good," Stone said.

Another cop in the Milo Hernandez Fan Club. Bray was going to figure that out at some point, just not right now.

"Why didn't you report this earlier? Get the FBI involved?"

"The kidnappers told me not to go to the police. And quite frankly, with Gary being a cop, I wasn't exactly sure who I could trust."

Officer Stone did not attempt to defend the police department. That was interesting.

"But they haven't made any contact with me. I had to take a chance on you."

"You did the right thing," Officer Stone said.

Bray stood up. "We need to know everything you know about Gary Blake. We understand the two of you aren't especially close coworkers and we'd like to understand that better. Anything that could help us identify who might want to harm him or his family."

Officer Stone looked from Summer to Bray. "There's information I can't share with you. But suffice it to say that it wasn't happenstance when I joined the Ravesville Police Department."

"I remember when you came," Summer said. "It was after Mary Michael's resignation."

"That was arranged," Officer Stone said.

Which meant that somebody had pulled some

strings to plant this man in the Ravesville Police Department. That was a significant investment.

"What do you know about my ex-husband?" Summer said. "About his disappearance?"

"From what I can tell, I think your husband was a decent cop at one time. Maybe never a good one but generally on the right side of the law. Then something changed about two years ago."

She'd divorced Gary about two years ago.

Bray could see the distress in her eyes. "Don't take this one on, Summer," he said.

"Probably good advice," Officer Stone said. "I think Gary made some bad decisions. Some recently and perhaps one or two a very long time ago," he added.

"What do you mean?" Summer asked.

"What do you know about a man named Brian Laffley?"

Chapter Fourteen

Thursday, 3:30 a.m.

Summer could feel the blood in her veins freeze. She'd never met Brian Laffley, but he'd changed her life. "Nothing," she said.

"Name doesn't mean anything to you?" Officer Stone pushed.

She shook her head. She hadn't talked about the man for fifteen years. She wasn't going to start now. "What bad choices did Gary make?" she asked, deliberately trying to get Daniel Stone off the topic of Laffley.

"Cards. Slots. Video poker. And I understand he's especially bad at the horse races."

Gambling. Financial trouble. That was consistent with some of the arguments she'd had with Gary. Money had become such a touchy issue with him. It was also consistent with Bray's comments when they'd been at Gary's house that it was odd that there weren't financial records around. He was taking steps to ensure that his secret stayed just that.

"And he's also turned a blind eye toward some drug trafficking that happens in and near Ravesville."

She felt sick. Even though they hadn't been married, she wished Gary had come to her. She would have tried to help him, tried to find another way to get himself out of the hole he'd dug.

"He's not dealing himself?" Bray asked.

"I'm not actually sure about that." Officer Stone rubbed the back of his neck. "Let me see your badge," he said.

That seemed to come out of nowhere. But Bray didn't hesitate. For the second time that night, he pulled out his wallet. He handed it to Officer Stone.

The man examined it. He drew in a deep breath. "In the spirit of collaboration, I'm going to share something with you. Don't put too much faith in Chief Poole's…ability to find your ex-husband."

"Ability?" Bray questioned.

"Ability. Interest. Commitment. Choose your own noun."

He was saying something without really saying it. And now Adie, sweet little Adie, with her thousand-watt smile and her bear hugs, could pay the price. "My daughter is missing, Officer Stone," Summer said. "I don't have time for innuendo."

"Chief Poole doesn't have your daughter," he said. "There's been someone sitting on him since we realized Gary was missing. I can't say anything else."

"Oh," she said, unable to keep her exclamation inside. This was getting so terribly complicated.

Bray got up, came around behind the couch and put a steadying hand on her shoulder. "Take a breath," he whispered.

She sucked in much-needed air.

"What do you know about his relationship with Sheila Stanton?" Bray asked.

"Not a lot of people know about that," Officer Stone said. "They were very discreet. This is probably not what I should tell the ex-wife, but I think he took the breakup with her hard."

SHEILA STANTON'S NAME had come up one too many times. "We plan on talking to her," Bray said.

"Good luck. I don't think you'll find her terribly trustworthy," Officer Stone said.

"She's a bad person," Lloyd chimed in.

He wasn't inclined to debate that, thought Bray. But how could he fault her for lying when he was fairly confident that Summer had just done the same thing when she'd said she didn't recognize the name Brian Laffley? The cop might have bought it, but Bray knew Summer much better, knew how she cocked her head to the right, just the slightest bit, when she was lying.

He didn't know Brian Laffley. He was sure about that. The name meant nothing to him. But it had meant something to Summer and to Gary Blake.

He liked Daniel Stone. And he'd had to talk to him for only about thirty seconds before realizing there was more to the man than being a small-town cop. When he'd admitted that he'd come to Ravesville for a reason, Bray hadn't been the least bit surprised.

He saw Summer stifle a yawn. She'd probably been up since four or five this morning, because the café opened at six. "Maybe you should make a pot of coffee," he suggested.

She nodded and got up. When she went into the kitchen, Lloyd followed her.

Bray waited until they were out of earshot. "Who is Brian Laffley?"

"*Was*, not *is*. Brian Laffley—that's not his real name, by the way—was a federal agent working undercover in this area for several months. There was reason to believe that a large and rather sophisticated counterfeit money operation originated near Ravesville. He disappeared one night. His body was never found. Of course a full investigation ensued but with no luck. That is, until about two years ago. A builder was excavating a site and a body was found. It was taken to the county morgue. Preliminary efforts to determine identity commenced, but when the coroner went back to finish the job the next day, the remains were gone."

Bray rubbed his temple. "I'm not sure I get where this is going."

"They said it was a mistake on the part of the funeral home. They had retrieved the body and already cremated it."

"Unbelievable," Bray said. "Honest mistake?"

Daniel Stone shrugged. "Funeral home said they got a call to pick up a John Doe. The people who worked at the morgue were intensely interviewed and none of them admitted making the call. We were playing catch-up the whole way because all of this happened before those of us in the know about Brian became aware that a body had even surfaced. We didn't know until the work that the coroner had done bubbled up through the system and then we were confident we had a match. It was Brian Laffley, and somebody went to great lengths to make sure that his body was destroyed."

"Cause of death identified?"

"Gunshot wound."

Was it possible that Brian Laffley had something to do with Blake's and Adie's disappearances? He'd told Summer earlier that it would be bits and pieces of information that would ultimately lead them to Adie. They just needed to figure out how all the bits and pieces fit together. It was getting more difficult by the minute.

But he appreciated that Stone had shared the information with him. He decided it was a good time to ask another question. "Earlier today, when Summer and I were leaving the café, there was someone across the street, on the second floor, watching the building."

"How do you know that?" Officer Stone asked, his tone decidedly more guarded.

"I saw his shadow."

"Really?"

Bray nodded.

"Well, Mr. Hollister, that tells me that you're pretty good. But don't worry about it. It has nothing to do with Adie's disappearance."

"If somebody is watching Summer's business, I want to know about it."

Officer Stone studied him for a long minute. "I know the person. He's not watching Summer. There's nothing to be worried about." A cupboard door shut in the kitchen. "Now, that's all I'm going to say," Officer Stone added. "And we never had this conversation."

Maybe the man had been watching Milo Hernandez, the ex-con. But if it wasn't Summer, Bray guessed he was good with it for now.

Summer and Lloyd came back, each carrying two cups. Lloyd gave one to Officer Stone and Summer gave him one. He took a sip. It was good.

Bray felt his cell phone buzz and he took it out of his pocket. It was Cal. "Yeah," he answered.

"Chase just finished up with his second place. He said it was a deserted gas station that hadn't pumped any gas since it was $1.67 a gallon. No sign of Blake or Adie but somebody had been there recently. There was a cigarette butt near the front door. We're at our third place right now. It's another deserted farmhouse. There was a fire. Either when people were living here or after they were gone. Can't really tell. No sign of recent activity."

That meant that a total of eight addresses out of the eleven had been searched and were big fat zeros.

"Thanks, Cal. Go home. We'll be in touch."

When Bray hung up the phone, he turned to Summer and shook his head. "Sorry," he said.

She nodded. "I think we need to tell Officer Stone about what we found. In the box," she said, somewhat cryptically, probably in the event that he didn't agree.

But he did. He pulled out the papers that he'd put into a large plastic bag at Chase's house. He opened the bag and carefully pulled out the top sheet. "Take a look at this," he said.

Officer Stone frowned. "What is that?"

"It's a list of addresses. We had to break the code. We found it in Gary Blake's safe-deposit box," Bray said.

"I didn't know he had a safe-deposit box," Officer Stone said.

"Me either," Summer admitted. "We found the key at his house."

"You searched his house?"

She looked him in the eye. "My mother cleans his house. She has a key and can come and go. She'd forgotten a mop there. I was trying to find it for her."

Officer Stone smiled. "Of course. I was there about noon," he admitted. "I didn't see the key."

"Did you check his boots?" Summer asked.

"I did. Shook them good."

"Did you put your hand inside?"

Stone smiled. "No, I did not." He looked at the papers. "All those have just one line?" Officer Stone asked.

Bray nodded.

"Can I see what you translated them into?"

Bray handed him the one-page document that he'd created with the eleven addresses. He watched the man scan the list. He didn't seem particularly interested in any of the addresses except one. "It sounds like you've got somebody checking these. Has anybody looked at this one?"

Bray shook his head. "Recognize it?"

"No. That's why I'm interested in it. The rest of these are all familiar."

That told Bray that he'd been right when he'd assumed the deserted sites were known drop-off points. But in rural areas, where a handful of officers were responsible for hundreds of miles, it wasn't generally a cost-effective means of waging the battle on drugs to stand guard over a particular location over a prolonged period of time.

If Officer Stone was interested in one particular address, then so was Bray. Especially because it was one of the addresses where there had been no result to the reverse-lookup inquiry. "We'll check it out next."

"I can do it," Officer Stone said.

Bray shook his head. "No police. We took a chance on coming to you and telling you the truth. Please don't make us regret that."

He could tell that irritated Officer Stone. That was tough.

"But," Officer Stone said, "I can help you. Let me."

Bray shook his head. "We can't take the chance. Right now, we're doing everything that the police could be doing."

"Maybe," Officer Stone said. "But you really

should contact the FBI. They have the experience to deal with this kind of thing."

They might have plenty of experience handling a traditional kidnapping where a ransom demand had been made. This was different.

"We're going to figure this out," Bray said. "I appreciate you letting me know that this address might bear looking into. If you hear anything, please call my cell." Bray rattled off the number. Officer Stone entered it into his phone. In turn, he gave Bray his direct number.

Bray turned in Lloyd's direction. "I assume that Lloyd isn't in any trouble for the 911 call."

Officer Stone waved a hand. "No trouble. It was pretty smart," he added. "I'll report back in that Lloyd was confused and close out the call. You two need to be careful. I know you're used to dealing with scum like this," he said, looking at Bray, "but don't underestimate them." He turned to look at Summer. "I hope you get your little girl back safe and sound. I've seen her when you've had her at the café. She's a little doll."

"Thank you," Summer whispered.

Officer Stone gave Bray another long look before shaking his head and leaving quietly.

Bray turned to shake Lloyd's hand. "Thank you."

Lloyd smiled. "I'll see you at dinner later. It's Thanksgiving."

Chapter Fifteen

Thursday, 4:30 a.m.

There was no name on the mailbox. Bray hadn't expected one, but he also hadn't expected that it would be a forty-minute drive on the back roads of Missouri only to find a gated estate, tucked into the hills.

It had been a scary last ten minutes. When he'd thought they might be getting close, he'd cut his lights. There was no need to advertise their arrival.

When he'd seen the ten-foot gate, he hadn't even slowed down as they'd driven by. There were no doubt cameras on the entrance, perhaps triggered by light or motion, and he wasn't giving anybody a good look.

Now, parked a half mile down the road, they sat.

"How do we get in?" Summer asked, her voice soft, as if someone might hear them.

"I don't know," he admitted. "This guy doesn't want unexpected company."

"It's certainly big enough to hide a man and a small child," she said.

"Yeah. But somehow it doesn't feel right. I mean, whoever owns this has big money. And based on what we know so far, it's a safe bet that they got it via illegal drugs. But it's clearly somebody's home. Do you bring that kind of stuff into your home? On Thanksgiving? When your family is coming?"

"We don't know that any of that is happening. Maybe he doesn't believe in Thanksgiving. Maybe he has no family."

"You could be right," he said. "The hell of it is, I'm not sure we can do much about it. If we try to approach, we're going to get intercepted, maybe shot. We can't take the chance. I won't let you take the chance."

"I have to," she said.

He was afraid that she was just about to make a break for it. He reached over, put his hand on her arm. "No."

"She's my child," she said simply.

"I know that, damn it. And I would move heaven and earth to get her back for you. But we can't just approach the gate and start asking questions."

"When we needed to talk to Daniel Stone, you

said we needed to find another way. We need to do the same thing now. Find. Another. Way." Her words were sharp. Insistent.

And he didn't want to tell her no.

But he was going to have to.

"Summer," he said, "we have to be—" He stopped. There was a flicker of light in the distance. He rolled down his window. There was a new noise in the predawn air. An engine.

A vehicle was approaching, and by the sounds of it, perhaps a truck. He listened for another thirty seconds. It was huffing and puffing up the hills, the engine whining. It was definitely a truck, and one badly in need of a tune-up.

Not likely owned by anyone who lived in this house.

But maybe by someone who did work at the house. Which meant that the gate would open and they would drive through.

Which might give him and Summer a chance to run through the gate on foot without being seen. A very slim chance.

"Let's go," he said.

"What?"

"There's nothing out here on this road but this house. So I'm making the assumption that that truck is coming here. When the gate opens, we might have a chance to sneak in."

She moved fast. And within minutes, they had

jogged down to the gate. The truck was closer now, maybe less than half a mile.

"Over here," he said, pulling her into the weeds across the road. They needed to avoid any spot that might get picked up by the truck's headlights. But they needed to be fairly close if they were going to run in behind the truck.

The lights came over the final hill, blinding them. But he could tell the truck was slowing. It turned into the driveway and stopped, the nose of the truck just feet away from the gate. The driver, a young man wearing a baseball cap backward, leaned his head out the window and pressed the button on the call box. "Morgan's," he said. "I got a delivery."

Was it even possible that at this time of the morning a vendor was delivering something to this house? On Thanksgiving?

Motioning for Summer to stand still, Bray moved far enough that he could see the side of the truck. *Morgan's Delicious Deli, St. Louis, Missouri.*

It looked as if the people in the big house were entertaining for the holiday and they'd decided to order in.

"Proceed." That from the speaker, near the call box. A man's voice. Then the gate started to slide open.

The young driver rolled up his window.

Bray heard the grind of shifting gears.

The gate was halfway open.

Soon.

They were taking their first step forward when the entire area was flooded with light. Bray dived for the ground, taking Summer with him. He covered her body with his. They were in deep grass that was sharp and dry, and the ground had a pungent smell.

He heard the truck move. Lifted his head just inches. Saw the gate closing. Felt the despair flood his system.

Five seconds after it closed, the lights went off, once again plunging the area into darkness. He helped Summer sit, then stand. "Are you okay?" he asked.

She didn't answer. She simply stared at the gate that was barely visible now even though it was less than ten feet away.

"We couldn't try it," he said. "It was too risky."

"I know," she whispered.

Even though she had to feel as if she'd got kicked in the teeth, she wasn't taking it out on him. She was amazing.

"What do you know about Morgan's Delicious Deli in St. Louis?"

"Nothing. I've never heard of it."

"Let's get out of here," he said. "We can look it up in the car."

They hurried back to the car and he started the engine to get the heater going. It was only about forty degrees outside and neither one of them had a heavy coat. With his lights still off, he pulled the car back onto the road, putting distance between them and the property. After he'd gone two miles, he finally turned his lights on and picked up speed. Ten minutes later, they were back on the highway.

He pulled off to the side again and used his smartphone. "Morgan's Delicious Deli has a small restaurant and a catering business for private parties. Upscale events. That's how they advertise it on the website."

"So if it's legitimate, it's as simple as somebody in the house ordered some food. Maybe they're having a big breakfast and everybody gets up early."

"If it's not legitimate, then maybe somebody was in the back of that truck."

"Maybe Adie," Summer said, her voice faint.

"That's a long shot," he said.

"I know," she admitted. "But I'm getting desperate. It's going on twelve hours."

"I think it's time to wake up your friend and get Sheila's address. We cannot ignore the fact that she left Ravesville, the place that she and her family have lived in for generations, just weeks before a man she's supposedly having a fling with disappears."

"I know. That seems odd but not any odder than the idea of Gary and Sheila being together. She…" Her voice trailed off. "Look, I don't really know her all that well, and at the risk of sounding like a jealous ex-wife of the new mistress, it's just hard for me to see her with Gary. She thinks a lot of herself. Maybe that's because of her family money. Maybe it's because she's very pretty. Gary just wouldn't be…enough for her."

But he'd been enough for Summer. That made absolutely no sense. He waited to see if she'd offer something more, but she didn't seem inclined.

SHE PULLED OUT her cell phone and scanned the numbers. Jacqui was a good customer. Her shop was just down the street from the café. She was forty-seven, fresh off her third divorce, and every day she had a new story about being single again in what was, to her, the new world of online dating.

It rang. A second time.

It was just after five. What were the chances that Jacqui was awake? Three times. Four. It would kick into voice mail soon. What the hell was she going to say?

"Hello," Jacqui said. She sounded awake.

"Hi. It's Summer Wright."

"Oh my gosh," the woman squealed. "I am so glad that I'm not the only one up at the crack of dawn defrosting my turkey. Who knew the little guy was going to be hard for so long. Wish my ex had had that problem."

Summer forced herself to laugh. "Mine's taking up most of the sink," she lied. "Hey, I won't keep you because I'm sure you're busy, but I was wondering if you'd have an address for Sheila Stanton."

Jacqui paused. "I do. But I guess I never thought that you and Sheila were that close."

"We were moving some booths at the café and I found a pair of really nice sunglasses that had fallen behind one of them. I remember seeing Sheila wear them. I thought she might appreciate having them back."

"I have her phone for sure and her mom gave me the street address of her apartment. But I don't have the apartment number." Jacqui rattled off the information.

Summer scribbled it on a slip of paper she pulled from her purse. "Thanks, Jacqui."

"No problem. I hear that cute Bray Hollister that you used to date in high school is back in town. Maybe you need to arrange a little Thanksgiving celebratory drink at the quarry. Unless times changed between when you and I went to high school, I'm betting you spent a night or two on a blanket out there."

Summer felt the heat start low and rapidly spread until she felt as if her face were burning. "Got to go," she mumbled and hung up.

She looked at Bray. Jacqui had a loud voice, and she was confident that Bray had heard every word.

"I got Sheila's address," she said.

"Uh-huh," he said. He took the paper from her and entered the address into his GPS.

Was he going to let it go? Could she be so lucky?

He put the car in gear. "I'm adding this to the list."

"What list?"

"The list of things we're going to talk about."

Chapter Sixteen

Thursday, 5:30 a.m.

They were quiet until they pulled into Sheila's condominium complex in the central-west end of St. Louis. The building was brick, eight floors. Nice enough but certainly nothing special. Cars were jammed tight along the street parking. It took two passes around the block before a car pulled out and Bray could take the spot.

Fortunately, when they'd left the Big House, as Summer had decided to call it, they were a third of the way to St. Louis already. They'd been able to finish the drive in about an hour. Still, Summer could feel her agitation growing with every second. When they finally got to the door of the building and she saw that it was a locked entrance, she wanted to pull her hair out. There were buttons to push to ring the residents, but none of them were marked for Stanton. There were two that were not marked with names, just with the apartment number. "She's probably not even home," she said.

"Let's find out," Bray said, pushing the first unmarked one. They waited. There was no response. He went on to the next one. Within seconds of pushing the button, a woman answered.

"Yes."

It was Sheila. Summer gave Bray a quick nod.

"Sheila, it's Bray Hollister," he said.

There was a pause on the other end. "*Bray* Hollister?" came the response.

"Probably hoping for Chase," Bray whispered. He pushed the button. "Yes. May I come up?"

Sheila didn't respond, but they heard the sound of the door releasing and Bray grabbed the handle. They took the elevator up to the fifth floor and knocked on 5B. Bray stood square in front of the door so that Sheila would be able to see him through the peephole.

Sheila opened the door. She was wearing red silk two-piece pajamas. The shirt buttoned up the front and the pants were wide-legged. The first three buttons of the shirt were undone, making it fairly obvious that she wasn't wearing a bra. When she saw Summer standing behind Bray, her expression changed from interested to irritated.

"Thanks for seeing me," Bray said.

Sheila shrugged. "I was curious," she said.

"And not willing to turn my back on an opportunity," she said suggestively. "But I'm not into sharing," she added, looking at Summer.

"Hi, Sheila," she said. "Would you have a minute that you could talk to Bray and me? It's about Gary."

Sheila's eyes didn't change, but her mouth did turn down at the corners. "It's pretty early to be visiting," she said.

True. But they hadn't awakened her. She'd been up. Her hair was brushed, falling perfectly straight, shorter in the back, longer in the front, angled toward her chin. Full makeup, including lipstick. She could not be human.

"Gary has been missing since yesterday morning," Summer said as they went inside and took a seat in Sheila's living room.

"I know."

Summer opened her mouth, then shut it. She was not exactly sure what to ask next. But luckily she didn't have to.

"My mother uses Chief Poole's wife's floral shop. She has a standing order. Fresh flowers in the foyer and all that."

She and Sheila had grown up in two very different types of houses. In the Wright house, they hadn't worried about having fresh flowers; they'd worried about having bread and were even more grateful when it was fresh.

"My mother ignores most of what the woman tells her but she did listen when it was about Gary. She was aware that we…had a brief entanglement."

It appeared that everyone had known about Gary and Sheila. It made her feel even more stupid that she'd missed it. She must have been the only one in Ravesville who hadn't known.

"What do you think about him being missing?" Bray asked.

"I don't think anything about it. Listen, I haven't seen Gary since I left Ravesville two weeks ago."

"And you haven't talked to him, either?" Bray pushed.

Sheila shook her head. She looked at Summer. "No offense," she said, "but what we had wasn't that much."

Summer couldn't care less what they'd had. But she wasn't walking away from Sheila if the woman had information that could be helpful. "This is important, Sheila. Do you have any idea where Gary might be?"

"Why is it so important?" Sheila challenged.

"My children are at risk," Summer said. "I can't say more than that, but I am absolutely confident that my children are at risk."

Sheila studied her. "Unfortunately, you may be right. I think your ex-husband has been hanging with people that you probably wouldn't want to have sitting at the counter of your little café. You and your sweet sister would probably find them objectionable."

"Why?" Summer pushed.

With one hand, Sheila pushed one side of her hair behind her ear. "Because even *I* find them objectionable," she said. "And my standards are questionable."

"What are they into?" Bray asked.

"I'm not really sure," Sheila said. She held up a hand. "Don't give me that look. I'm not stupid. I didn't want to know. I overheard a phone conversation, okay? And I could tell that the person on the other end wasn't happy about something. When Gary got off the phone, he was really agitated. He tried to laugh it off but I knew it was something."

"What did the other person say?" Bray asked.

"He said he wanted his money."

"When was this?"

"Maybe three or four weeks ago."

Was it possible that Gary had gambled away such a large amount that he was, as they say, borrowing from Peter to pay Paul? Had he borrowed from the wrong people and they weren't interested in an IOU?

"Did you tell Gary to break it off with them?" Summer asked. Had Gary got sideways with some bad people because he was trying to make his new girlfriend happy, trying to keep her from leaving?

"I did not," Sheila said. "Gary and I were..." Her voice trailed off. "Gary and I were never going to be a long-term thing. I knew that. I thought he did."

He probably hadn't. Gary was obtuse when it came to relationships. Their marriage had been over for years before she'd finally asked for a divorce, and still he'd been terribly surprised. But that wasn't the important thing right now. "Was it drugs?" Summer asked. "Was that what Gary was involved in?"

Sheila stood up. She was clearly done with them. "Drugs. Prostitution. Money laundering. Gambling. List all the vices you can think of. I'm not sure which one these people were involved in. All I can tell is that whatever it was, it's not good."

"Don't you think it's a strange coincidence that Gary goes missing shortly after you leave Ravesville?" Bray said.

"My mother said the same thing," Sheila said. "I think she was actually a little worried that I might have done something. You see, Gary didn't take the breakup well, thought he could convince me different if I'd just listen. He was becoming a bit of a stalker."

Had Gary been so intent upon changing Sheila's mind that he'd done something crazy? Done business with the wrong people?

"The thing between Gary and me was probably a mistake," Sheila said. "And I hope that nothing bad has happened to him. But it's not my fight."

Bray looked at Summer. The message was clear. They weren't getting anywhere.

"I'm sorry we bothered you," Summer said.

Sheila didn't answer.

They were at the door, almost through it before she spoke.

"If it helps, Gary was talking like he was going to have a pile of money really soon. I think he thought it would make a difference to me."

Bingo.

"Would it have?" Bray asked, his tone sarcastic.

She shook her head. "Not enough money in this world."

His brain was going down a path and it didn't look good for Blake. If Blake was dealing drugs, then he was collecting money that ultimately had to be paid to the higher-ups. Was it possible that he'd been stupid enough to gamble that money away and then try to tell the boss that he was a little short?

People ended up in the river wearing cement shoes when they pulled that kind of stunt. Or with a bullet in their head.

And that could explain Blake's absence, but it didn't explain why the kidnappers needed Adie.

The only explanation was that they were trying to convince Blake to talk. About what?

Damn. He felt as if he were trying to fit a square peg into a round hole. Bray resisted the urge to slam his car door. He knew that Summer had to be as frustrated, and he was the one who needed to stay positive.

He was pretty confident that Sheila Stanton wasn't lying. She probably was the type to take a hands-off approach toward anything that had the potential to affect her negatively. When she'd figured out that Gary was hanging with a bad crowd, she'd cut bait quickly.

She hadn't, quite frankly, cared enough about Gary to try to pull him back, to protect him.

"Now what?" Summer asked.

Bray looked at the clock. It was going on six. Starting to get light. Twenty-four hours ago, Summer had been unlocking the front door of the café, never dreaming how bad her day was going to become. She had to be exhausted. She had a pinched look around her pretty mouth and there were dark circles under her eyes. "You need to get some rest," he said.

"I can't rest." She stared out the side window, still looking at Sheila Stanton's building. "Besides, you have to be just as tired as I am."

"There are times on the job that I don't get much sleep. I'm more used to this."

She shrugged. "I just need some coffee. Maybe some toast."

It was Thanksgiving, but someplace had to be open for breakfast. It wasn't sleep, but caffeine and food would be better than nothing. He started the car and pulled away from the curb.

"We need to go back to the Big House," she said. "We have to find a way to get in and search that property. We can't leave it undone."

It was possible that they'd see a way inside that hadn't been clear in the dark. And he had to admit that his gut was also telling him that that location was important. It was a fortress in the middle of nowhere. Why?

To keep people out or to keep them inside?

For the first time since this whole thing had started, he drove aimlessly, his mind working on the possibilities. Up one street, down another. There were cars parked on both sides of the street but very little traffic.

What was the best way to get in?

Maybe it was time to ask the police for help. Regardless of the instructions they'd received, maybe it was time to bring in other resources.

They could get a search warrant. Might be a little more difficult today, given that it was Thanksgiving, but a child was missing. People would move quickly.

And Adie might pay the price for that.

Nervous kidnappers were a scary thing. He turned the corner.

And almost ran into what might be a solution.

Chapter Seventeen

Thursday, 6:00 a.m.

The delivery truck for Morgan's Delicious Deli was parked at the end of the alley, its back end jutting out far enough that it caused Bray to swerve to avoid hitting it.

The driver, the one who had pushed the button on the gate, was wheeling an empty cart toward the building to the immediate left.

Morgan's Delicious Deli had its lights on and was open for business. Bray took the first available parking spot. "Let's hope they have coffee."

Summer turned to him, her eyes excited for the first time in hours. "Are we going to ask them about the Big House? Ask them what they saw there?"

"I don't know," Bray said. "Let's play it by ear."

Even though he wanted to storm the place and demand answers, Bray strolled in, holding the door open for Summer. There were only two other customers, a man and a woman, in the small eating area. The place had a clean tile floor, three wooden booths along the front window and four other small tables. Along one wall was a counter with stools for additional seating. The wall was a mass of electrical outlets. Customers could bring any one of their many gadgets and be assured of a place to plug it in.

There was a big refrigerator with glass doors where customers could help themselves to a selection of water and juices and prepackaged salads. The room smelled of raisin toast.

A woman, probably late thirties, wearing a white chef's coat, was behind the counter. "Number six," she said, pushing a tray of food forward. The man at the table got up and fetched the food, grabbing a bottle of ketchup off the counter before he headed back to his table. Bray paid him no attention.

The cooking area and food-prep areas were protected by a chest-high counter, but the truck driver had entered by a back door and was now in the kitchen, opening refrigerator doors and pulling out silver trays topped with plastic wrap.

The woman turned her attention to Bray and Summer. "Good morning," she said.

"Morning," Bray said. "Boy, were we happy

to see that you were open, with it being Thanksgiving and all."

She smiled. "Three hundred sixty-five days a year," she said. "Leap year can't come too soon," she joked. "What can I get you?"

"Coffee and whole wheat toast," Summer said.

"Same," Bray added, pulling out some cash. "I never thought about getting the whole Thanksgiving feast catered," he said easily. That was a lie. That was exactly what he and Chase had usually done when they'd shared Thanksgiving dinner.

The woman handed him a brochure with a plump roasted turkey on the front. "Maybe for next year. We'll take care of everything," she said. She gave Bray his change, poured two cups of coffee into thick paper cups and handed one to each of them. "I'll get your toast," she said.

Bray and Summer took the table closest to the counter. Bray sat so that he faced the kitchen. The woman had put four slices of bread into a big white toaster and stood in front of it. She was talking to the man. Her voice was low. She didn't look happy.

He watched her pick up a list and it appeared she was checking off items. Then she looked in the refrigerator that the man had been pulling trays from and pulled one more. The man put all three of them on his cart and wheeled it toward the back door.

"Are you sure you have everything this time?" the woman asked, her voice louder.

The man nodded, looking contrite. "I'm sorry about that, Greta. I didn't realize that there was cold food in addition to the hot items."

"It's fine." The woman's voice softened. "I just wish it wasn't a hundred miles there and back. But it's worth doing the return trip. We don't have many like the Pataneros account."

Return trip. One hundred miles there and back.

Bray looked at Summer. She nodded, telling him she understood. The driver was headed back for another delivery to the Big House. He heard a *pop* and the woman turned to butter their toast. She looked over her shoulder at the driver, who now had the back door open. "You want some breakfast before you go back out?"

The man considered. "Maybe a cup of coffee and one of your cinnamon rolls. I'll eat on the road. Let me get these in the truck and I'll be back for it."

The woman finished buttering Bray's and Summer's toast and put two slices each on two small plates. "Number seven," she said.

Lucky seven, thought Bray. "Can we have those to go?" he said.

"Sure." She opened a foam container, dumped all four pieces into it and slid it across the counter.

Summer waited until they were outside before she whispered, "What's going on?"

"Keep walking toward the car," he said under his breath. Once they were inside, he took a sip of his coffee and watched the truck driver exit from the back of the truck. "Get ready," he said. "We're going to have to move fast."

"Move where?" she demanded.

"That driver is going back to that house and we're going with him."

"With?"

"Yes. In the back of the truck." He winked at her. "Any questions?"

She seemed to consider. "Yeah. Can I bring my coffee?"

THE MINUTE THE man was back inside the deli, they were moving. Walking fast, not running. At the truck, Bray turned the handle and it swung open. It was dark and cold inside. It was a big step up and she hiked up her skirt to take it. Bray followed her in and pulled the door closed.

"What if he comes back?" she said, wrapping her arms around herself. "What if he forgot something else?"

"We have to hope that doesn't happen. Let's get as far back as possible. If he has to shove something else in, hopefully he'll open the door quick, get it settled, and he won't see us."

"What if he does?" she asked.

"Then I'm going to distract him long enough for you to get out and head for the car. Then I'll catch up."

"What are we going to do when we get through the gate? When he opens the door there, we'll be in an even worse position if he sees us."

"Don't worry," Bray said. "I'll figure something out."

Don't worry. That was all she'd been doing since she'd been bumped at the mall. "I wish we could see what was going on," she said, her voice low.

"I know. Here—eat your toast."

"You brought it?"

"Of course. It's a forty-five-minute ride. You need something to do," he said confidently. He pulled his keys from his pocket and turned on the mini flashlight. "These don't look too bad," he said, nodding his head at the two trays of fresh fruit kebabs. "Kind of fancy," he said. He looked at the third tray. "Salmon and capers. Whatever happened to oatmeal for breakfast?"

She laughed, just couldn't help it. And it felt so good. They were stowed away in the back of a truck, about to be discovered at any minute, and he wanted to talk food.

She stopped laughing abruptly when they heard

the driver's door open. Felt the driver sink into his seat. Heard the engine turn over.

Felt the truck start to move.

She sat down quickly to avoid falling down and realized that it was going to be difficult to keep from crashing into things. Bray followed her to the floor.

Before she realized what he was doing, he sat behind her with his legs extended and pulled her tight into his body.

She started to resist.

"Let me keep you safe," he said.

Bray Hollister always did have a way with words. She settled back into his chest, loving the feel of his strong arms wrapped around her, his chin resting on her head.

Stowed away in the back of a strange truck, no doubt about to be discovered, she felt safe.

Amazing.

She ate her toast and drank her coffee, and then she closed her eyes.

And didn't open them again until Bray was gently shaking her. He leaned close to her ear. "Wake up, honey. We have to be very close," he said, "and the truck is slowing down."

"Did you sleep?" she asked, stretching her neck.

He shook his head.

Of course not. He'd been watching over her. "Tell me what we need to do," she said.

"We're going to have to get out while the truck is still moving," he said. "It's the only way. Based on what I could see last night, once the truck gets through the gate, there's a long drive that curves at least once before it reaches the house. It's uphill and there's a sharp curve, so he's going to have to slow way down. That's when we make our move."

She nodded. She was going to jump from a moving truck. Well, okay.

Her fear had to pale in comparison to what poor little Adie had endured. Still on her bottom, she scooted closer to the door.

The truck stopped. She heard the driver announce himself. Then the muffled crackle of someone on the other end, granting them admission. She couldn't hear the gate—it moved too smoothly. But the truck was inching forward, picking up speed, then slowing.

Bray held out his hand, helped her stand. Then he kissed her hard.

"Big jump," he said and unlatched the door. "Bend your knees when you land. Nothing to it."

Chapter Eighteen

Thursday, 7:30 a.m.

She didn't have to jump because Bray, with a hand on each of her hips, literally tossed her out of the back of the truck. He hadn't warned her because he hadn't wanted to scare her. But he'd also intended that she end up as close as possible to the tree line at the side of the road.

She was still in the air when he jumped, knowing that it wasn't going to be possible to shut the door that had swung wide open. Which meant that when the driver got to the house and went to unload his truck, he was going to find the door open.

Hopefully the guy would simply thank his lucky stars that nothing had fallen out, causing him to make yet another trip back to this location.

He saw Summer hit the ground. She bent her knees too much and pitched forward, onto all fours. He hit the ground a step behind her, scooped her up with his hands again on her hips and literally pushed her into the trees.

He grabbed her hard to stop their forward momentum. Her face was white and she was breathing hard. Her palms were scratched and one finger had a small cut, likely from landing hard on a rock.

"Are you okay?" he asked, checking her for other injuries.

"Did he see us?" she asked, ignoring his question.

"I don't think so," he said. "He'd have stopped the truck pretty fast. Let's just hope that if there are cameras on the road, nobody is watching the screens." He grabbed her hand. "Let's go. We need to work our way up to the house."

The fall foliage was still damp, likely from rains earlier in the week. It didn't snap or crackle, but it was hard to see the dips and holes, and several times he had to pull on Summer's hand to keep her from falling.

It was crazy of him to bring her here. He should have demanded that she stay behind.

She'd have hated him for that. He was too damn much of a coward to risk that. But now he was risking her life.

He could see the house now. It was huge. No other word for it. A sprawling two-story with a main house and wings off to both the east and the west. Red brick. White pillars. Circular drive.

Pretty fancy for rural Missouri.

The Morgan's Delicious Deli truck was parked in front. The engine had been turned off. The back door was open but the driver was still sitting in the cab of the truck.

Bray was close enough now that he could see the driver had his cell phone in his hand and was texting someone. Hopefully it wasn't 911.

"Now what?" Summer asked.

Getting inside the gate had been a huge accomplishment but would be for naught unless they got inside the house. "I've got an idea," Bray said, "but you're going to have to stay here, out of sight."

"I don't like the sounds of this," she said.

The driver opened his door.

Damn. "I don't have time to explain," Bray said. "You have to stay hidden. I texted Cal while you were sleeping in the truck. He and Nalana are driving here right now, in two separate vehicles so that they can leave one for us. He knows we're going to try to get inside." Bray looked at his watch. "He's expecting another text in twenty-five minutes, at eight o'clock. If that doesn't happen, he's going to know something is wrong and he'll get help."

The driver was walking to the back of his truck. He was going to see the open door any second.

"But—"

He kissed her. "Don't show yourself, no matter what happens. Promise me."

She nodded.

He took a step.

"Bray," she said, her voice a whisper.

"Yes."

"I need you to know. I never stopped loving you."

Bray felt his heart lurch in his chest. He'd been waiting years to hear something like this.

Out of the corner of his eye, he saw the driver stare at the open door, his hands on his hips. Then the man stepped into the back of the truck.

It was now or never.

"Same for me, Summer," he said. "Exactly the same."

WHEN THE DRIVER got out of the truck with a tray in his hands, Bray was standing on the sidewalk. "Hey, thanks for coming back," he said, using his East Coast accent to the max. "My sister really appreciates it."

The driver nodded. "No problem. Our mistake," he said.

"Let me help you with those trays," Bray said, holding out his hands. They weren't shaking, which was a damn miracle since Summer had picked about the worst possible time to drop her bombshell. *I never stopped loving you.*

"I can get them," the driver said.

"I insist," Bray said. *Get your head in the game, Hollister.*

"Well, thanks," the driver said, handing off the tray he held and turning to step back inside the truck for another.

Bray slowly let out his breath. Working undercover for so many years had taught him that sometimes you had no choice but to simply act as if you belonged there.

It was going to get tricky fast if somebody opened the front door. But it stayed shut, and soon the driver was back with a second tray. Bray motioned for him to proceed.

"Same place as before?" the driver asked.

"Yes," said Bray.

The driver didn't head for the front door. Instead, he walked toward the wing that extended eastward. He opened a big wooden door that led into a breezeway of sorts that connected the wing to the main house. Bray thought it looked like the lobby of an expensive hotel. The floor was marble, the walls were covered in textured wallpaper, and there was a piece of art perched on an easel that probably cost what he made in a year.

At one end of the elaborate space, there was a door. The driver opened it and they were in a big kitchen that had enough stainless steel to make a restaurateur green with envy. There were two side-by-side refrigerators with glass fronts. The driver opened one of the doors and slid his tray inside. Once he was done, Bray stepped forward and bent his knees so that he could put the tray he was holding onto the shelf directly below. He was just straightening up when he heard a noise at the door. He turned and saw a woman, thin, all in black, probably midthirties, in the doorway. Her dark hair was in a ponytail. She was looking at the driver.

"I told Tom that if you hurried you'd make it back in time. He got upset for nothing. I'm sorry about that. It's just that breakfast on Thanksgiving Day has always been his deal."

"Totally understand," the driver said. "I'm just really sorry, Mrs. Pataneros, that we didn't get it right the first time."

Bray said nothing. The woman hadn't even looked at him.

"No harm done. Everyone is just starting to gather anyway. I put the egg casseroles in the oven on low just like you said."

"Great. I've got one more fruit tray and that will do it," the driver said. He started walking out.

Bray followed him. The woman gave him a half smile, like one that people gave to strangers when they weren't sure what to say to them. He did the same in response and kept walking. Ten steps into the breezeway, he glanced over his shoulder to verify that the woman hadn't followed him. The driver was almost at the door.

He took a sharp right and headed up the wide, shiny wooden stairs to the second level.

SUMMER WAS COLD and the only thing she could do about it was wrap her arms around herself. She had on her jean jacket, and while it had been plenty warm the night before, it hadn't been sufficient for an hour ride in a refrigerated truck, nor for standing in wet grass, when the morning temperature was midthirties at best.

She should have been, at the very least, warm from embarrassment. She'd told Bray that she'd never stopped loving him. Why the hell had she done that? Not that it wasn't true, but why admit it now? To him?

Because she couldn't bear the thought of him never knowing it. And she was confident that there was danger inside this house. When Bray had walked up to the truck, as though he had every right to, her heart had almost stopped.

He was taking a great risk. For her. For her child.

Was it any wonder that she'd never stopped loving him?

But was it too late?

It didn't matter how much she loved Bray if Adie didn't come home safe. She would never be able to forgive herself or forget the horrible situation that had brought them back together.

She saw the driver come back outside. But no Bray. What the hell was he doing in there?

The driver carried in another tray. He didn't seem concerned that he'd lost Bray somewhere.

Now he was back, hands empty. Shutting the door of the truck, checking to make sure it was latched tight. Then he was in his vehicle. He started the engine and came around the circle driveway, headed straight toward her.

She kept perfectly still, knowing that it would be movement that attracted the man's gaze. Time seemed to crawl by, but it was only seconds before he was past her, on his way back to St. Louis and his own Thanksgiving dinner.

She looked at her watch. Bray had been inside for eleven minutes. What the hell was she going to do if he didn't come out? He would expect her to work her way toward the gate, to get to the vehicle, to get away. Could she leave him? How could she not if it meant that she would still be free to look for Adie?

The toast in her stomach rumbled and her legs felt weak. She contemplated sitting down.

Instead, she drew in a deep breath. Then another. Bray would come back. He would not leave her. Not willingly.

BRAY WAS IN the upstairs hallway when he had to quickly duck into an empty bathroom. Voices, louder now, coming closer. A man and a woman, talking about Black Friday shopping. Her excited, him resigned.

Now they were past.

He counted to five, then poked his head out. The wide hallway had thick beige carpet and was in the shape of an L, with doors on both sides. The couple had come from the section that he couldn't get a visual on. He moved forward, intent upon starting at the back and working his way forward.

He did not encounter any more people, but it was obvious that three of the four very large guest suites were occupied. When he was done, he was comfortable that neither Adie nor Summer's ex was in that section of the house. At one point, he looked out of one bedroom window, trying to see Summer. But even knowing where she was, he couldn't spot her.

If somebody in the house had discovered her and they touched one hair on her head, he was going to kill them all.

He moved fast, knowing that he needed to cross into the main house and search it and the other wing before he could go. The second floor of the main house was rectangular in shape, with two bedroom suites on each side and the whole rear of the house dedicated to a media room and a well-stocked library.

Only one of the four bedroom suites was in use. He suspected the owner of the house liked his privacy and made sure his guests were comfortable in the more distant wings.

He could hear voices, one talking over the other. The family had gathered below, anxious for their breakfast egg dishes and smoked salmon. Silverware clanked against plates. Someone laughed too loud. His stomach growled in response to the smell of cinnamon drifting up the open staircase.

He moved toward the remaining wing. It was set up exactly like the other. It did not take long to search all the rooms, although he had a bit of a start when he opened one door and a young male, naked to the waist, was stretched across the bed. He was sound asleep and there was an odor in the room that was part sweaty teen and part marijuana smoke.

Maybe he'd stumble down by the time they pulled the turkey out of the oven later today.

Bray finished his search. He knew there was no need to search the first floor. With this many people in the house, nobody would be brave enough to keep two kidnapping victims that close. But he found himself hesitating as he contemplated the best way to exit the house. There was no basement, not unusual even for expensive houses in these parts.

He'd seen Mrs. Pataneros, but he really wanted a look at her husband, wanted to see the man who saw fit to put this kind of opulence in the middle of nowhere. Wanted to be able to describe him to Summer, just to make sure it didn't mesh with anybody that she knew.

He went back to the main section and slowly descended the stairs, thankful that it was quality workmanship and there wasn't a single squeak. He eased around a corner. The dining room was huge, probably eighteen by thirty, and there was a long table that took up a fair portion of the room. He counted. Seven on one side, six on the other, one at each end. If Sleeping Beauty upstairs had made it to the table, there would have been sixteen.

They were all listening to a young girl of maybe ten years old talk about her horseback-riding lessons. He could see the man at the head of the table and assumed it was Mr. Pataneros. He was very tall and very thin and did not fit Summer's description of the kidnappers or the video from the mall. He swallowed his disappointment and was about to turn away to make his final escape when the man to Mr. Pataneros's right turned his head.

Bray saw the port-wine stain on his face. He barely had that processed when the man across the table lifted his hand to reach for the fruit kebabs and Bray caught the sparkle of a gold ring with black filigree and a big red stone.

A ring big enough that it could be seen under a pair of thin cotton gloves.

The man with the ring reached over and rubbed the girl's head. "So proud of you, Victoria," he said. "You did all that yesterday and still managed to get to breakfast on time. More than I can say for your brother," he added, frowning at the empty chair.

"Let it go," said a woman with hair the exact same shade as Victoria's. "He got home safe last night. That's what matters."

Bray wanted to bust in, shove the kebab down the man's slimy throat and demand answers, but he didn't. Years of training kicked in. He would not risk Adie's safety for the short-lived pleasure of inflicting some pain on these two.

Very quietly he walked from the main house into the east wing, where he had entered just thirty-six minutes ago. He opened the door, walked out, but before he disappeared into the tree line, he did one more thing.

Then he moved fast, working his way back to the spot where he'd left Summer.

Only she wasn't there.

Chapter Nineteen

Thursday, 8:10 a.m.

Summer heard the men's voices before she saw them. They were walking up the paved driveway, conversing in Spanish. Both were dressed for outside work in blue jeans, flannel shirts and insulated vests.

Both carried shovels.

And her heart started to race. It was Thanksgiving Day. What would someone need a shovel for?

To dig a grave.

She put her hand over her mouth, afraid that she might not be able to keep her anguish silent.

She had to follow them. She had to know.

They did not head for the house. Instead, they turned down the road that led to the right. She waited until they got a hundred yards away before she started to follow them.

It meant she had to cross the road. That couldn't

be helped. She was going to have to take the chance that if no one had seen them jump out of the back of the truck, then nobody would see her now.

Stepping carefully so as not to make a sound, she kept them in sight. Every ten steps or so, she would pause and listen. At one point, she realized that the sounds had changed.

And so had the smell of the air.

Horses.

Another fifty feet and she saw the circular riding corral and the long white stable. The men had entered, leaving the big doors at one end open.

She felt relief course through her body. They weren't burying bodies. They were mucking out horse stalls.

She felt her cell phone buzz in her skirt pocket. It was a text from Bray. Where are you?

She texted back. Approximately 1300 feet east of where you left me. She'd been counting steps and she was walking toward the morning sun.

Stay there, came the reply.

Within minutes, he was there. Holding her close. He was shaking.

"You scared me," he whispered in her ear, "when I couldn't find you."

"I saw two men walking. With shovels."

She saw the understanding in his eyes. He knew what she'd been thinking.

"We have to get out of here," he said.

"Did you find anything?" she asked.

He nodded. "I think so."

Now it was her turn to shake. "What?"

"I'll tell you everything. But first, we have to go. I'm going to text Cal and let him know that we'll be on the road in three minutes."

She had a thousand questions but she kept them to herself as she hurried behind him. When they got to the edge of the property, Bray motioned for her to stay in the trees. Then he ran across the road, entered the guard shack, and suddenly the gate was sliding open like magic.

He motioned for her and she ran for all she was worth. They were still running two hundred yards later when they saw Cal's SUV over the hill. Bray reached under the front right wheel well and came out with keys.

Then they were inside and moving fast. Bray pressed on the accelerator, navigating the rural road with confidence.

She looked over her shoulder. No one was chasing them. Yet.

Bray was watching the rearview mirror. She knew he was likely worried that somehow the gate opening had tripped some kind of alarm in the house.

"Tell me everything," she said.

He tossed her his phone. "First, there are pictures of the license plates for all the cars that were parked at Pataneros's house. Forward them to Chase. He'll be able to run the plates and get us a name and address of the owner."

She did so and set his phone back onto the middle console.

He took his eyes off the curvy road just long enough to make eye contact. He explained about the people in the suites and the young male who had been asleep and smelled of marijuana. "Port-wine-stain guy is there," he added.

She grabbed his arm, so fast and so hard that the vehicle swerved to the side. "We have to go back. Now."

Bray shook his head. "I searched the whole house. I don't think Adie and your ex are there, so it would do us no good to go back."

But that man, that awful man, had to know where Adie was. Summer wanted to shake the truth out of him. No. She wanted to beat it out of him. She wanted to hurt him. Badly.

The intensity of the hate that she felt almost overwhelmed her. It threatened to take her under, to keep her from being able to think, to plan.

She stared into Bray's eyes. *Help me* was her silent plea.

"This was a big break, Summer," Bray said. "I think I might have seen the other man, as well. He was dark-haired, light-skinned, and wearing a big gold ring with lots of black filigree and a big red stone. I'd be willing to bet that's the ring you saw under his black gloves."

Gold ring. Lots of black filigree. Big red stone. She let those words roll around.

"What?" Bray demanded, still watching her eyes.

"I've seen a ring like that before."

"On who?" Bray said quickly. "Do you have a name?"

"I do, but it doesn't make sense. Well, maybe it does."

"Tell me."

"Several years ago, I went to an office Christmas party with Gary. Chief Poole hosted it at a restaurant in Hamerton. It was a fancy place. We got dressed up."

"Someone there wore a ring like this?" Bray said.

She nodded. "Yes. Chief Poole. He told me it was his college ring."

BRAY CONSIDERED THAT. "From the beginning, we thought that whoever had committed the crime had some way of knowing if you followed directions and contacted police. You would have either gone to Poole or perhaps to the FBI, who would have notified Poole out of professional courtesy, and either way, he'd have been in the loop."

"But he was the one who told us that Gary was missing. He questioned us."

"Yeah. And his investigation was perfunctory at best. I gave him a pass, figured he was a small-town cop and didn't have any experience with this kind of situation. I think he questioned both of us because it would have seemed really odd if he didn't. After all, Reverend Brown and Poole's sister-in-law Julie had overheard our exchange in the church basement. But when he talked to me, he didn't even take notes."

"With me either. Let's assume he had to do something," Summer said, "once Officer Stone had stopped by Gary's house and seen the mess and reported it. He couldn't ignore it because he knows how information flows in a small town."

"I agree. I suspect Poole wouldn't have done anything about Gary's absence. But since someone else had noticed, he had to play the part of the concerned employer who just happens to be local law enforcement."

"But Officer Stone said they had people on Chief Poole, watching him. He was confident that he hadn't kidnapped Adie."

She looked so hopeful that he hated to break the news to her. "Unfortunately, Summer, I think it's possible that Poole is involved in this up to his neck. He may not be the one who kidnapped Adie or your ex, but I think he probably knows something about it. This has to be big. Very big. Kidnapping is a federal offense. If he's in any way an accessory to a kidnapping charge, he knows he's going to do some serious prison time. Cops don't do well in prison. I suspect he'd rather die."

"What do we do?" she said, her voice ragged.

"Tell me about Poole. What do you know about him?"

She ran her fingers through her hair. "Not much. I know he came to Ravesville about four or five years ago. Gary was mad that he didn't get a promotion to chief at the time, but the mayor and Gary weren't close and he ultimately had responsibility for the decision. It was tense between Gary and Chief Poole for a while, but then that changed and they seemed to be getting along better."

"Sheila said he was married."

"Yes. Like Sheila says, his wife owns a flower shop in Hamerton, so I didn't see her very much."

Flower shop. Independent business. Deliveries coming and going at all times of the day, nobody paying attention. "So they're probably closed today."

"Sure." She turned to look at him. "Oh my gosh, Bray. You think they're at the flower shop?"

"I don't know. But we're not that far away and we should check it. What's the name of the flower shop?" Bray asked. He was driving very fast.

"I don't know. I was never there. But I know it's

on the main street that runs through town. There can't be more than one."

"Let's hope not," he said, his tone curt.

"What?" she said, looking frightened. "Bray, there's something you're not telling me. I know it. You have to tell me all of it. I can't bear not to know."

"Honey," he said. He wanted to stop the damn car and pull her into his arms, but there was no time. "I've told you everything."

But he hadn't. He hadn't told her about the young girl relating the story about riding her horse or about how her father had sat there, making a big show out of listening to his daughter's tale, all the time knowing that he'd taken someone else's daughter. It was driving him crazy that he didn't know if the man was able to eat his eggs without fear of heartburn because he hadn't harmed Adie or because it was over.

There was no way he was going to tell her that it was possible that they were too late.

When they got to Hamerton, it didn't take them long to find the flower shop. Poole's Pansies and More was in the middle of the block. There was a big closed sign in the front window.

He drove past, made a right and took another sharp right into the alley that ran behind all the businesses that lined the main drag. There was one parking space by the back door. It was empty.

She expected him to pull in, but he didn't. He continued on, three more businesses, finally pulling in between the red pickup truck and the black Toyota that were parked at the Laundromat.

They walked back to the flower shop. "I don't see any security cameras," Summer said.

"Maybe we'll get lucky," Bray said.

SHE HAD FORGOTTEN that he was carrying lock picks. Was it really just a little over eight hours since she'd seen him pick the lock on that very first ramshackle house? It seemed like a lifetime ago. But again his skills were handy. The door opened within seconds.

And then the alarm started ringing. It was loud and it hurt her ears. "We're going to have to hurry," Bray yelled.

How could she even think? There were small tables with plants and candles and inexpensive gifts. A big refrigerator was against the wall, and in it were several vases of fresh flowers. On the bottom shelf was a bucket of carnations.

It looked like every other small flower shop she'd ever been in. There was no sign of Gary or Adie. "Is there a basement?" she asked.

Bray shook his head. He was standing in the middle of the room, simply looking around.

"What are you looking at?" she demanded. Her hopes had been raised and, again, stomped on.

"For anything that doesn't look quite right," he said.

She closed her eyes, took a deep breath, opened them again. Surveyed the room.

Flowers in the cooler. Check. Plants near the sunny window. Check. Bulbs in bins by the door. Check. She walked toward the back room where there were two worktables that were probably three feet wide by six feet long. On one, more than twenty pots with brightly colored poinsettias sat ready. After Thanksgiving was over, those would probably be moved to the front. Check.

On the other table were… She stepped closer. Grave-site markers, some round wreaths and some in the shape of a cross, all decorated with silk flowers. She stared at the one at the end closest to her. She'd seen one just like it last night, when they'd been wandering around the graveyard. That made sense. Funeral flowers and burial-plot decorations were probably big business for flower shops. She was just about to turn away when she saw the two pots, half filled with dirt, at the far end of the table.

That didn't make sense. You wouldn't pot plants in dirt in the same area that you were arranging silk flowers. She got close and tried to lift the pot. It was too heavy. She could dump it, maybe, but then there would be dirt everywhere. But she didn't want to walk away from it. She took off her jacket, rolled up her sleeve and plunged her hand into the dirt all the way up to her elbow.

And she felt something besides dirt. She got a grip and pulled her arm out.

In her hand was an envelope full of cash. Stuffed full of hundreds and fifties. Thousands and thousands of dollars.

"Bray," she screamed.

He came fast. Saw the cash, the messed-up dirt, and didn't even bother to roll up his own sleeve before he stuck his arm into the remaining pot. He pulled out a matching envelope.

They'd been inside for almost two minutes. Time was running out.

"Now what?" she said.

In response, Bray walked up to the counter and pulled a blank sheet of paper out of the printer. He picked up a black Sharpie, too. He wrote his cell-phone number in big letters, folded the paper and put it back into the second pot. Then he patted the dirt down in both pots.

"I don't know why I was worried about security cameras," she said, shaking her head. "I didn't realize we were going to leave a card."

He smiled. "It's time for them to come to us. Let's go," he added, putting both envelopes of cash in his coat pocket. He opened the back door and out they went. They hurried down the alley and got into their vehicle.

They were out of the alley, back on the main drag, before they saw a police car round the corner.

Chapter Twenty

It was a Hamerton police car with one officer. Bray didn't speed up or slow down. The cop's eyes were totally focused on the flower shop. He was probably wondering how long it would take him to figure out how to shut off the alarm.

He figured Poole and his wife wouldn't be far behind. If the alarm system worked like most, they would have got a call from the alarm company. That would have spurred action. The alarm company, upon learning this was likely a real event, would have dispatched local police, and Poole and his wife would have jumped into the car. But they lived in Ravesville, which was a twenty-minute drive.

Bray intended to be long gone before they arrived.

Poole and his wife would notice right away that

the money was gone. It was doubtful that they'd tell the Hamerton police. Hard to explain that kind of cash hidden under some dirt.

But once they got the Hamerton cop out the door, Poole would no doubt use the police resources at his disposal to try to find out whom the cell number belonged to. But he wouldn't be successful. One of the benefits of being an undercover DEA agent was that his cell-phone number was registered to a fictional Frank White in Boise, Idaho.

Then Poole would have no choice but to call the number.

This was about to get very interesting. And while he might enjoy screwing with Poole for a while, the stakes were too high. Adie had been gone for sixteen hours.

Summer could not be expected to take much more.

So he was going to squeeze Poole hard and fast.

"What is Poole doing with this kind of money?" Summer asked, sounding a little dazed. "And is this the same money that Gary thought was about to fall into his lap?"

"I don't know. But I'm starting to think that there's more to the relationship between Poole and your ex than anybody knows. It's not your typical boss-employee thing."

"I don't see Gary as a drug dealer," Summer said.

He bit back a sharp reply. How could she still believe in the man?

She held up a hand. "I know what you're thinking," she said. "That I have blinders on when it comes to Gary. I don't. I know that he's not perfect. But I just don't see him as a drug dealer."

Bray knew way better than most that drug dealers came in all sizes, shapes and colors. Bank executives with penthouse apartments in Manhattan, housewives in Brooklyn, gang leaders in the Bronx. All kinds of people, some you might automatically suspect and some you'd never dream of, were making a ton of money. As a result, the money that moved through legitimate commerce as a result of illegal drugs activity was staggering.

And made it a damn difficult war to fight.

"It's possible that he was investigating something," Bray said, hardly believing that he was offering up a solution that would exonerate Summer's ex.

She didn't respond for several minutes, but he could tell she was thinking. They were back on the highway, headed toward Ravesville. His phone should be ringing any minute.

Summer shifted in her seat. "Maybe Gary was blackmailing Poole."

Now, that was interesting. "Why would you think that?" Bray asked, careful to keep his tone neutral.

"It…it seems like something he might do."

"Because...?"

"Because he's done it before."

THE MINUTE THE words were out of her mouth, she wanted to take them back. But in her heart, she knew it was time. Past time. Bray needed to know the truth.

The car was slowing fast and Bray made a quick turn onto a side road. He drove until he had crested the first hill so that he was no longer visible from the highway. He pulled off to the side of the road and put the vehicle in Park. Then he turned toward her. "That's quite a bombshell," he said. "I think I need to hear more."

She could put him off. She could tell him that she just couldn't do this right now because of her concern for Adie. And he'd back off. Because he was that kind of guy.

A good guy.

Whom she'd let believe a lie for fifteen years.

She drew in a breath. "When you enlisted in the Marines, I intended to wait. I meant what I'd told you."

He said nothing, but she could tell by the set of his jaw that he was prepared to hear something difficult.

"My mom always drank too much. I knew that when I was a ten-year-old. But after my dad died, it got worse. You were gone then, so you didn't see it," she said.

He nodded. "I always felt bad that I wasn't able to get home for his funeral."

"I understood. Anyway, after that, she was really bad for a few months. Then she seemed to want to change. Over the next year, she tried a few different programs. Unfortunately, she failed all of them. Trish was basically done with her but I still had hope. And then something terrible happened."

She had never told anyone about this. And now she was about to tell the person it had hurt the most.

Well, not the most, perhaps. That would have been the dead man. And his family.

"What?" he asked softly.

"She was driving home from the bar. It was late. She hit a pedestrian and killed him."

"Who?" Bray asked.

"His name was Brian Laffley."

"Stone asked you about him," Bray said, his voice hard. "You said you didn't know the name."

"I lied. I've been lying for a long time." She swallowed hard.

"What happened?"

"Gary was the cop on duty. I knew him, of course. He'd moved to town just a year or so earlier. In a small town, everybody knows the police. Especially when they're young and sort of handsome. Lots of my friends had a crush on him. And, well, he'd asked me out a few times."

Now she could see the anger in Bray's eyes. She knew what he was thinking. He'd been off fighting a war and she'd been messing around with the new guy in town.

"I didn't go," she said. "I always said no. But unfortunately, I think maybe that made me more interesting. Maybe more of a challenge."

"You've always been a beautiful woman," Bray said. "He'd have been a fool not to have been interested."

He wasn't going to be giving her compliments when he'd heard it all.

"Gary brought my mother home that night. Trish was on a date but I was home. Mom was a wreck, just sobbing. It was her third DUI and she'd killed someone. She was going to prison."

"He brought her home?"

Summer nodded. "Yeah. Not exactly proper police procedure. But then again, nothing was proper about that night." She stared at her shoes. "Gary said that he could make it all go away. That he would get rid of the body. That Mom wouldn't be arrested, wouldn't be charged with any crime."

She looked up, into Bray's eyes. He was so smart. He knew what was coming. "If?" he prompted.

"If I married him."

BRAY GRIPPED THE steering wheel, trying to come to terms with what Summer had said and then tying it together with what Officer Stone had said. It was a bad horror movie with images coming at him from all directions.

Summer thought her mother had killed someone. And she'd allowed it to be covered up. That meant she had been willing to be an accomplice to a homicide. That was one blinking light at the edge of his vision.

But her mother hadn't hit Laffley and killed him. Officer Stone had said that it was a gunshot.

It all came back to Gary Blake.

Had he killed Brian Laffley? Had Summer been married to a killer? When he'd said that he could make it go away, did that include getting rid of Laffley's body? But had he screwed that up, too?

When he somehow became aware that Laffley's body had resurfaced, did he orchestrate the mix-up at the funeral home?

The only thing he knew for sure was that he'd used Laffley's death to entrap Summer into marriage. And Summer had let him.

And hadn't trusted Bray enough to tell him the truth when he'd come home just months later.

For years, he'd believed she simply didn't love him enough.

He wanted to punch something.

"Bray," she said.

He cut her off. "No. Don't say anything else. Not just yet." He felt as if he couldn't get enough air. He opened his door. Fumbled his way out of his seat belt and out of the car.

Stood perfectly still in the chilly, quiet morning air and drew in a breath, then a second one. He felt the cold air burn his lungs, clear his head. He got back into the car. Turned to her.

"You need to know something," he said. And then he told her about his conversation with Officer Stone.

She listened, not saying a word. When he was done, she shook her head. "That's not possible. My mother saw the man. Saw him crumpled up next to her car."

"She was drunk. She probably didn't inspect the body. I suspect that she probably passed out and your ex found her. Then he either drove her car to where Laffley's body was or he moved Laffley's body to where your mother was. Somehow, he connected the two events."

Her eyes widened as what he'd said sank in. "You think he shot Laffley?"

"I have no idea. Maybe he did. Maybe he was involved in something bad and discovered that Laffley was a federal agent and decided that he needed to disappear. Or maybe he was a cop on duty and discovered a dead man? Then when he saw your mom, it was simply fortuitous. Either way he did something really wrong. He either murdered a man or concealed the murder of a man."

She started to cry. And she couldn't catch her breath. She wrapped her arms around her stomach and her body shook with loud, racking sobs.

Was she crying for the son of a bitch? Was she worried that he was going to go to jail? It was more than he should be expected to take. Before coming back to Ravesville, he'd have sworn that Summer Wright could never do anything to hurt him again, that she'd broken him once but now he was immune.

He'd been wrong.

But still, he hated to hear her cry. Through all this, she'd been steady, but this was the thing that had pushed her over the edge.

Was it even possible that she still felt something for her ex? He opened his car door because he felt sick.

"Oh, Bray," she said, sniffing. "I don't—" she swallowed "—blame you for leaving. I am...so sorry." She hiccuped. "I hurt you so badly. For nothing. I'm so sorry."

She wasn't crying for her ex. She was crying for him.

"Aw, honey. I'm not leaving. Ever." He closed his door, pulled her into his arms and held her. He patted her back until she was spent and her head drooped on his shoulder.

Finally, she lifted it. Her eyes and nose were red and she looked very weary. "What do we do now?"

"We put this aside," he said. "Laffley is dead. Has been for a long time. We focus on finding Adie."

He picked up the two envelopes of money and started counting. He was almost done when his cell phone rang. He looked at it, recognized the number. "It's Chase. After we find Adie, we'll sort the rest out," he said, finishing his earlier thought. He swiped his phone and clicked the button so that it was on speaker. "Yeah," he said.

"I've got the information you wanted on the license plates," Chase said. "The BMW is from Chicago. I did a little quick research. The man is Pataneros's brother. The other two, the Lexus and the Camaro, have the same address. Same last name. Pitard."

That made sense. The young man who had smelled like pot probably drove the Camaro and his parents drove the Lexus.

"I couldn't find any connection between them and Pataneros," Chase said.

"I think I might know the connection. It's to Chief Poole. I suspect they might have been college buddies," Bray said, glancing at Summer. "What's their address?"

"8713 Bluehound Road."

Bluehound Road. Bray reached for the list of properties they'd searched. "One of the abandoned properties was on Bluehound," he said to Chase.

"I know. At 5211 Bluehound. The two places are a couple miles apart. I'm guessing several tax brackets, as well, based on the vehicles and that they're friends with Pataneros."

"I think you're probably right," Bray said. Something didn't make sense but he couldn't put his finger on it.

"You want Cal or me to check it out?" Chase asked.

"No." If Poole was working with Pataneros, they needed to make sure that they had Pataneros and his friends wrapped up tight before word got to them that Poole had been taken down. They might blow away in the wind. And Adie might never be found. "I've got Cal watching Pataneros's place, seeing if anybody moves. I'm on my way. Join me there. It's time to figure out what these guys know."

"We'll need to be careful," Chase said.

Bray understood. If things went south fast and Pataneros and the other two were killed, the trail to Adie would disappear.

"We will be," Bray said. "I'll be there as fast as I can, maybe twenty minutes."

Bray turned to update Summer, but before he could, his phone rang again. "It's Poole," he said.

Chapter Twenty-One

"You left a number, so I'm calling," Poole said.

"I appreciate that," Bray said. When he'd talked to Poole yesterday, he'd poured the East Coast on thick. Now he wiped it from his delivery, staying Midwest all the way. He wanted to make sure that Poole didn't know whom he was talking to. "I thought you might want to talk about the money."

"I don't like talking about money with strangers," Poole said.

Bingo. "You can call me John."

"John what?"

"Just John," Bray said.

"You're messing with the wrong people," Poole said.

"Messing with some rich people, you mean," Bray countered.

"What do you want?"

"I want in on some of the action. This is a lot of money, but I've been watching you. You cover a lot of geography. I don't think that's fair."

There was a pause on the other end of the line. "I'm not sure I know what you're talking about," Poole said.

Bray picked up the sheet of paper with the addresses. "Really. Well, maybe this will jump-start your memory." He rattled off the address of the cemetery.

Now there was an even more pronounced pause. Bray resisted the urge to fill the silence. He could see that Summer was moving in her seat and she was clenching and unclenching her hands.

"Well, then," Poole said, "I'll ask one more time. What is it that you want?"

"I want a meeting with your boss."

"Why?"

"Because I want to discuss business with him. Quit asking stupid questions," Bray said.

"Well, you know, it's Thanksgiving."

Bray started to whistle. Off-key. Stopped after a few bars. "If you want me to blow the lid off your little organization, keep talking crap."

"I'll give my boss a call," Poole said.

"You do that. But don't make me wait too long," Bray said. He hung up.

"Oh my God," Summer said. "What are you doing?"

"I'm getting your daughter back," he said, starting the car.

"How?"

"I know all kinds of people like Chief Poole. To generate this kind of cash, he's got to have a big-time operation going. He is not going to let some punk weasel his way in. He's going to want to deal with me quickly and efficiently, but first he needs to figure out if I'm working alone or if I've shared any of what I know with someone else. You can automatically assume that he thinks he's three times as smart as me. He's going to try to find a way to get his money back and shut me up. For good."

"I wish we knew how Gary fits into this," Summer said. "Whether he was part of it or simply trying to cash in and they decided he was a bug that needed stepping on."

"We'll know soon enough," Bray said. He, quite frankly, didn't give a damn about Gary Blake. Through his duplicity, he'd changed a lot of lives, Bray's included.

"About what I told you," Summer said.

"Not the right time," Bray said.

"But—"

Bray's phone rang. Bray let it ring three times before he answered. "Yeah."

"He's agreed to a short meeting."

"Fine. There's a park in Ravesville. I'm sure you know it," Bray said.

"No. We'll meet you at 1403 Hazel Road."

Bray quickly glanced at the list of addresses on his sheet. It didn't match any of them. "Where is that?"

"Get a map," Poole said, his tone sharp. "And be there in an hour." He hung up.

Bray punched the address into his GPS. It was northeast of Ravesville, about fifteen miles. From where they were right now, it was a thirty-minute drive.

He dialed Daniel Stone. When the officer answered, Bray didn't waste any time. "By now, if you really have people sitting on Poole, you know that he's moving. He went to his wife's flower shop in Hamerton. Now he's headed for 1403 Hazel Road. He thinks he's meeting me. He's anxious to do that because I removed about $200,000 from a couple flowerpots. I'm not sure what you all have been waiting for, but I think it's time."

Officer Stone laughed. "We've been waiting because we couldn't find the damn money. Thank you. Where are you?"

"I'll let you know." Bray hung up. It was time to join Chase and Cal.

Chapter Twenty-Two

Thursday, 9:43 a.m.

Adie had been gone for more than sixteen hours. Summer desperately needed to hear her child's voice, feel her small arms around her neck, smell her little-girl smell that was some unique combination of shampoo, peanut butter and strawberry lip gloss.

Now that it seemed as if they might be close, she was more frightened than ever. What if they were too late? What if Adie was...?

She couldn't bear to think the word.

Bray had turned the car around and was headed back to the main road. When he got to the stop sign and started to turn right, she put her hand on the wheel. "Stop," she said.

He didn't shake her off even though she could tell that he was impatient to move forward. "What?" he asked, his tone calm.

"When you searched Pataneros's house, you said that it was clear that everyone had spent the night."

He nodded.

"Have you ever met a friend for an early-morning breakfast?"

Now he was looking at her as if she'd lost her mind. "I have."

"So did you go over the night before?"

Bray shook his head.

"It doesn't make sense that Pitard and his whole family spend the night at Pataneros's house when their own house is less than ten minutes away. Why wouldn't they simply just get up early and drive over?"

"Maybe they did something together last night. You know, they started celebrating early."

"You said the one kid who was sleeping reeked of pot. I don't think they were doing that as a family activity."

Now Bray started strumming his thumb against the steering wheel. "The wife said that Thanksgiving Day breakfast was always a big deal to Pataneros. I suspect the good wife is oblivious to how her husband makes all his money. But she would think something was very odd if suddenly he didn't want to have the Thanksgiving Day event, especially since the food was already ordered. And he probably always has his brother and his best friend and their families join him. Tradition. That's what Thanksgiving Day is. You eat the same food with the same people, year after year."

"But this year they had a problem," Summer said.

"Yeah. Your ex. If they took him, they would need a place to stash him."

"If you lived nearby, you might take your family to your neighbor's house the night before if there was something going on at your own house that you didn't want your wife or kids to see," Summer said.

"Exactly." Bray picked up his cell phone.

"What are you doing?" she asked.

"I'm going to get a visual of Pitard's house." He punched some keys. In just seconds, he was handing her the screen. The image was amazingly clear. Pitard's house was not as lavish as Pataneros's house but it was still probably over a million dollars, in a part of the country where somebody could get a real nice place for $200,000. It was a two-story colonial, white with black shutters. There was an attached three-car garage with all three doors down. There was an in-ground swimming pool and a couple of acres of yard, surrounded by trees on three sides.

"Very isolated," she said.

"Yeah, no neighbors around to hear much of anything."

She pointed at the screen. "Those are basement windows," she said.

"I think so," he agreed.

She felt sick. "What should we do?"

Bray didn't answer. He simply cranked the wheel and took off fast toward Pitard's house.

"Do you think it's possible," she asked, now breathless that she'd put forth the possibility, "that Adie and Gary are there?"

Bray pushed the accelerator to the floor and the car was flying down the road. "We'll know in ten minutes," he said.

THE MORE HE thought about it, the more certain Bray became that Summer was onto something. Thank goodness she'd put it together. There'd been something nagging at him that told him that something wasn't right with what Chase was telling him about the addresses, but quite frankly, he wasn't really trusting his instincts right now.

Summer had not loved Gary Blake. She had married him to keep her mother out of jail.

Yet she'd had two children with him. That stung. "Can I ask you something?" he said. He should be concentrating on driving, but he couldn't wait another minute.

"Of course," she said.

"I get that you married your ex because you were trying to help your mom. But you had Keagan and then Adie. I'm not sure I get that."

"And I stayed married to him for a long time."

Her tone said it all. She understood what he was asking.

"Once I had made the decision to marry Gary, I was determined to make the best of it. He told me over and over again how much he loved me, and I thought if I tried hard enough, I could love him, too. I got pregnant with Keagan almost immediately, and having him…well, that strengthened my resolve to make my marriage work. Gary was good with his son."

She stopped. Bray remained silent.

"After a few years, I knew that I was never going to love Gary. Not like he wanted to be loved or professed to love me. I… I had been in love. I knew what it felt like. And that wasn't what I felt for Gary."

Bray felt as if he had an elephant sitting on his chest. He gripped the steering wheel hard, letting his emotion have some small physical outlet.

"When I tried to talk to Gary about it, he always told me that he was patient, that he could wait for me to really love him. And for years we drifted along like that, but I had pretty much made the decision that I was going to have to leave. Then when Keagan was eight, Gary arranged for us to go on a honeymoon. We'd never taken one and he booked a week at an all-inclusive resort in Mexico. I almost told him no, but he was so excited about it, said that he thought it might make a difference between the two of us."

"Did it?" Bray asked.

"Well, it did, but not in the way you might think. I was taking birth control pills to prevent the possibility of another pregnancy and I thought I'd packed my pills but they weren't in my suitcase when I arrived. Gary saw that I was upset and immediately went to the small store at the resort and bought other protection."

She turned to look out the window. "I got pregnant with Adie on that trip. And so help me God, I didn't want to be pregnant. I didn't want another baby." She paused. "Maybe I'm being punished for that now."

"No," Bray said. "That's not how it works."

"After I had Adie, I stayed with Gary for another year or so but I just couldn't do it. I told him I wanted a divorce, and the kids and I moved into an apartment that Trish helped us get."

"How did he react?"

"He was angry and he let it slip that he'd thought another child would make the difference. That's when I realized that he'd deliberately taken my birth control out of my suitcase. For all I know, he poked holes in the condoms, too. But I couldn't be mad about having Adie. She was a delight from the day she was born. I will never regret having either her or Keagan. It wasn't a marriage of love, but something wonderful, two somethings, came out of it. I can't regret that."

"What I witnessed in the church wasn't a happily divorced couple," Bray said.

"I know. For the first two years after our divorce, Gary was very cold to me. He took the kids on his weekends and he paid child support, but there was very little interaction between the two of us. Then it got really weird. He stopped paying child support. When I told him he needed to, he warned me that if I pushed it, he was going to tell the truth about what my mother had done."

"He would have implicated himself," Bray said.

"I know. I told him that. He said that he'd deny it. He said that he'd hidden the body but would make sure it was found and that my mother's DNA was all over it. I didn't know if he was telling the truth and my mother never had any memory of what really happened that night. So I stopped asking for support. Gary started to see the kids less and less, but when he had them, he was good with them. I never worried about that."

Bray looked at the GPS. They were within a mile now of Pitard's house. He slowed down. He didn't want to have to deal with Gary Blake right now. But he really, really wanted to bring Summer's little girl home. And he probably wasn't going to be able to do one without the other.

If they were in the house, he was going to do everything he needed to do to get them out of there.

But he wasn't going to do it without Summer knowing the truth.

He pulled the car off to the side of the road. "Summer, there's something I need you to know."

She swallowed hard. He could see the delicate muscles of her throat working. "I don't expect you to ever be able to forgive me," she said.

He reached for her hand. It was cold. "I fell a little bit in love with you when you were sixteen and you dipped your French fries in mayonnaise on our first date and gave the waitress at that seedy little bar and grill a five-dollar tip because the table next to us stiffed her. I thought, this girl is different. And then when you were seventeen and used your prom-dress money to pay for a lawyer for your mom because she'd gotten a DUI, I knew I had something special. And when we made love for the first time at Rock Pond, I knew that I wanted to make love to you until I was ninety."

"Oh," she said, her eyes filling with tears.

"When I enlisted, I knew it probably wasn't fair to expect you to wait. But I wanted you to. Desperately. And when I came home and realized my life was never going to be what I had hoped and dreamed about all those long nights in a faraway desert, I was angry."

He stroked his thumb over the light blue veins in her small hand. "But I never, ever stopped loving you. I'm not angry anymore. You did exactly what I would have expected you to do. You took care of your mom the way you'd been taking care of her since you were a kid. You tried to make the best of a bad situation. You've been doing that since you were a kid, too. You said you don't expect forgiveness. There's nothing to forgive, Summer. There's only love. I love you."

And then she was in his arms. And he was kissing her. Her lips, salty from her tears, had never been sweeter. "I love you, too," she said, her mouth close to his ear. "I always have. I always will."

"Then let's go get your daughter," he said, praying harder than he'd ever prayed before that Adie was safe.

WHAT THEY HADN'T been able to tell from the online picture was that the house was not visible from the road. There was a narrow blacktop lane, a mailbox with the address stenciled on in gold letters, with an attached black plastic sleeve designed to hold a newspaper. Somebody had delivered the *St. Louis Post-Dispatch* that morning but nobody had picked it up yet. There was no security gate or visible security cameras. Pitard had kids. That would have likely been a big hassle with a family that was always coming and going.

"We walk in," he said.

He parked the car off to the side of the road, near where the yard ended and the trees started. Then they walked up the hill, staying very close to the tree line. When they crested the hill, they could see the house.

It looked very much the same as the online photo except that, today, there was a light green Maxima in the driveway.

Exactly like the light green Maxima that had got gas courtesy of the men who had abducted Adie.

He held up a hand, stopping Summer. Then he pulled out his cell phone and pushed the button that he'd entered into his phone while they'd been eating BLTs in the kitchen.

"Dawson Roy," the man answered.

Chase's partner with the St. Louis police department. Chase had made contact with him at Bray's request, put him on notice that they might need some police assistance quickly.

"Dawson, this is Bray Hollister. I'm at 8713 Bluehound Road in Ravesville. I need immediate backup."

"My pleasure, Bray," Dawson said. "My friends in the state police are ready to rock and roll."

Bray hung up. "I think it's always a good idea to have a backup plan."

"Thank you," she whispered.

The man inside would most certainly be armed. Bray had his own gun in his hand. But Summer was not armed. Vulnerable.

"You won't consider staying here," he said, as they stopped forty feet from the house.

"No," she said. "Adie has only seen you twice. She'll be frightened. She needs to know I'm here."

"Just be careful," he said. "Whoever is here is probably going to shoot first and ask questions later." Damn, this sucked. They'd just found each other after all these years and now there was danger that could rip them apart.

He just couldn't let that happen.

"We're going to try to enter through the garage and get inside the house that way. People forget to lock their interior door all the time," he said.

But that was going to be harder than he'd hoped when he tried the side door of the garage and found it locked. "We're going in through there," he said, pointing at the window next to the door. He was ready to break it with his flashlight when he realized that there was just a little gap between the window and the frame. It was one of those types that cranked out, and when somebody had

closed it, they hadn't latched it from the inside. If
he could get his fingers inside and pull it open, it
might just work.

"Let me," Summer said, seeing what he'd seen.
"My fingers are smaller." They were, and it took
her just seconds to open the window.

He listened for an alarm but didn't hear anything. "Let me go first," he said. He got in and
turned to help her. Once she was inside, he pointed
at the two empty spaces in the cold garage. "I bet
a Lexus and a Camaro go there." There was a
workbench with some tools. He picked up a heavy
wrench and handed it to Summer. "You played
softball in high school. I know you've got a hell
of a swing." Then he saw the roll of duct tape and
put it in his coat pocket.

There was the door that led to the house. "If
they're here, I'm betting they're in the basement,"
he said.

She pulled at his sleeve. "Please try not to shoot
anyone. I don't want Adie to see that."

She was killing him here. "I'll do my best."
He opened the door, edged around the first corner. Motioned for Summer to follow. It was the
kitchen. A sterile-looking room, done in black and
white with all stainless-steel appliances. There
wasn't even a dirty dish on the counter. It didn't
look as if anyone even lived in the house. From
there, they searched the rest of the first floor.

There was a formal living room, a dining room, a bathroom and a more casual family room. In this room, there was an open staircase that led to the basement.

He listened. And thought maybe he could hear a television. Yep. Somebody was watching the Thanksgiving Day parade.

He took the first four steps. It was a finished basement, probably where the kids hung out.

But not today.

Two more steps. He could see the flat-screen television now. It was on the far wall.

Two more steps. He could see almost the whole room. There were couches and chairs and…there he was. The guy watching the parade. He had a bag of chips on his lap, a beer in his hand and a Glock 27 on the table next to him.

Bray took the remaining four steps, walked up behind the guy and put his gun to his temple. "Happy Thanksgiving," Bray said. "Don't move."

The guy's leg twitched but that was it. Bray motioned for Summer to get the duct tape from his pocket.

He handed her the gun. "Pull the trigger if he moves," he said, loud enough for the man to hear. He got in front of the man, tossed the chips aside and set the bottle of beer on the table. Then he quickly tied the man's wrists together, then his ankles. He took his gun back from Summer.

"Know him?" Bray asked.

Summer shook her head. She was staring at the two doors. One right next to the other. Both shut.

Bray took one last look at the guy. He was probably somewhere near the bottom of the pecking order. Low enough that he got to do guard duty on Thanksgiving Day. Bray took the heel of his palm and knocked it against the man's forehead. His head snapped back. "You better hope that that little girl is okay," he said.

Then he opened the first door. Gary Blake's arms were stretched over his head, his wrists tied to the bed. He wore his pants and a white T-shirt. His eyes were closed. The man's face was barely recognizable. He'd been beaten badly and there was lots of blood on his shirt. Bray heard Summer gasp.

Gary opened the one eye that he could. Saw Summer. "Adie," he croaked.

"We'll get you help," Bray said. "Hang on."

Summer was already moving toward the other door. She opened it before he could get to her. He heard another gasp.

Chapter Twenty-Three

Thursday, 10:05 a.m.

Summer saw her little angel sitting on the bed, propped up against a pillow, a book in her lap. She was wearing the same clothes that she'd had on at the mall.

"Mama," she said. "I missed you."

Summer stumbled into the room and wrapped her arms around her child. She pulled her tight.

"Daddy's hurt," Adie said.

"I know, honey," Summer said. "We're going to help him. Don't you worry about anything."

In the background, she could hear Bray talking. He was on his phone.

"Are you hurt? Did they hurt you?" she forced herself to ask. She ran her hands down her little girl's arms, her legs. Cupped her sweet face in her hands.

"No. But I'm hungry," Adie said. "They said

I couldn't see Daddy again until breakfast. Is it time for breakfast?" she asked, looking up at the ground-level window and seeing the light.

"It is, yes. And I'm going to make you the best breakfast ever," Summer said, sniffing her tears back. "You can wear your new shoes." She would not cry and scare her child any more than the poor little girl had been scared. "And you can see your dad in just a little while."

Bray stepped forward. "Let's get the two of you out of here. I just talked to Dawson again. There's an ambulance on the way."

"I need to talk to Gary," Summer said. "Can you stay here with Adie?" Thus far the little girl did not seem overly traumatized by what had happened to her father and to herself, but Summer definitely didn't want her seeing Gary in that condition.

"Make it fast," Bray said. "Nalana is on her way to get you and Adie out of here." He turned toward Adie. "Can you show me the pictures in your book, Adie?"

Summer slipped out of the room. Bray had cut the rope that had tied Gary to the bed and Gary was awkwardly rubbing his shoulders. "I'm sorry this happened to you," she said.

"How's Adie?" he asked quickly.

"I think she's okay."

Gary closed his one eye and sighed. He looked like a small, deflated man.

"They said they were going to kill both of us when they got back if I didn't tell them what they wanted to know."

"Why the hell wouldn't you just tell them, Gary? How could you put your daughter through this?"

Again, he opened the one eye. "You must really think I'm a son of a bitch," he said, his tone raspy. "I would have done anything I could have to save Adie, to protect her."

"Then I don't understand."

"I couldn't tell them what they wanted to know because I didn't know the damn answer."

"I don't understand."

"It's complicated."

"I think I deserve to know," she said.

He sighed. "You know some of it. It started with Brian Laffley."

"I know my mother didn't kill him."

"How…how long have you known that?"

"For about an hour," she said.

He shook his head. "Well, then, I wish I'd had the opportunity to tell you myself. You know, a man has a lot of time to think when he's waiting for somebody to come back and kill him, and I'd made the decision that if Adie and I did manage to escape, I was going to tell you the truth."

Oddly enough, she believed him. "Did you kill Laffley?"

"Of course not," he said. "For God's sake, Summer, what I did was wrong. I should never have pretended that your mother hit him. I should never have coerced you into marrying me. But I'm not a killer."

"What happened?"

"I knew Laffley. He'd been in town for a few weeks, living at that run-down hotel at the edge of Ravesville. I thought he was a bum. I'd encountered him a couple times and he always smelled like alcohol. I was working nights then. I took a stroll through the park and found him. He'd been shot. I was just about to call it in when I got a radio call about a vehicle parked on the street. Based on the description, I knew it was your mom's car. I put two and two together and I guess I came up with five."

"Why?" she asked. "I just want to know why."

"Hell, Summer, I don't know. I'd been asking you out for months and you would never say yes. You were the prettiest, nicest girl in Ravesville and I... I was just Gary Blake. I wanted what I couldn't have and I found a way."

"Brian Laffley's body surfaced about two years ago and then disappeared from the morgue. Did you do that, too?"

He shook his head. "I knew the body had been

found. And I knew the coroner was looking at it. I didn't realize it was missing until I heard that everybody at the funeral home was getting questioned. I was dating Maggie Reynolds."

"How…? Never mind." She had forgotten that Maggie had taken a job as a secretary at the funeral home after she left the library.

"You know, she was the one who took the call from the coroner's office. The instructions were to pick up the body and dispose of it immediately. But everybody at the coroner's office was denying that they made the call. Maggie was really upset about it. Besides the guy who found the body, there were only two people who knew about it. Me and Chief Poole. I didn't make the call. It had to be him. The only reason the chief would have had to get rid of Laffley's body was if he was responsible for killing the man. I think he panicked."

"But Laffley died years before Chief Poole came to town."

"I know. I would never have connected it if he hadn't made the call. Poole was a grunt on the St. Louis police force at the time of Laffley's death. But I think even then he had business dealings in Ravesville. Bad business. Probably something that involved Pitard and Pataneros, who were living here. Not sure what it was, but something bad enough that he got crosswise with a federal agent."

"You never told Poole what you knew?" Summer asked.

"Nope. But things were starting to make sense. You see, I'd stumbled across a pretty big drug drop and had arrested a guy. But then suddenly, the evidence was missing and there was no case. I pretended that I didn't care. Sometimes," he said, looking a little ashamed, "it helps to have a reputation as a lazy cop."

He sat up on the bed, holding his ribs. "I put a tracking device on Poole's car. Everywhere he went, I knew about it. It didn't take me long to figure out his favorite places or the schedule for deliveries. I'd be waiting there before he showed up. Poole wasn't at the bottom of the food chain, handing off drugs to the end user. He was higher up, a firmly entrenched middleman."

"You should have reported him," she said.

He grimaced. "I intended to. But… I wanted him to sweat first. He never should have had that job. It should have been mine. I started sending him anonymous letters, letting him know that someone knew."

She could hear the sounds of approaching sirens. Bray had no doubt let them know that he had the bad guy subdued and there was no need to come quietly. In just minutes, Gary would be taken away.

"The people who did this to you. Were they acting on Poole's orders?"

"No. Poole worked for them, not the other way around."

"That makes no sense."

Gary moved and grimaced. "Damn. I think they broke a couple of my ribs."

She did not have it in her to feel sorry about that.

"I think Poole figured it out," Gary said. "He told his friends who were also his bosses that I knew and that I was going to go to the authorities. He also told them that I'd stolen a whole lot of money from him, money that Poole owed to them. That's what they wanted from me. Money. And I kept telling them that Poole had it, that he was the one who was trying to screw us all. But they just kept talking with their fists. I got to the point where I started to not care if they killed me." He looked up. "But when they showed up with Adie and said that they would kill us both if I didn't tell them where the money was, I…I couldn't believe it. I love that little girl. You know I do."

She heard the sound of a door opening, footsteps up above, then on the stairs. "I know you do, Gary. And for what it's worth, I'm glad you're okay. But if you ever, ever do anything like this again, that puts my children in danger, I'm going to kill you myself."

Then she walked out of the room, ready for the rest of her life.

Epilogue

Thursday, 6:00 p.m.

The Hollister house hadn't had this much activity for some time. His mother would have been delighted to see her old dining room table laden with food and the chairs full of family. Chase stood, ready to carve the turkey. Raney sat next to him. Then Cal, Nalana, Lloyd Doogan and Flora Wright. Bray took the far end and to his left was Summer, Adie, Keagan, Trish and Milo.

Family. Friends. Joy.

Not for everyone. And rightly so. The Pataneros brothers were in custody, along with Pitard and the man at his house. Poole, too. It would take a while to sort out, but Bray was confident that for the foreseeable future, their holiday meals were going to be served in a prison cafeteria.

Summer's ex was in the hospital and then would face his own set of legal challenges for what he'd done to Laffley's body. Suffice it to say, he'd never work as a cop again.

Bray reached for Summer's hand. This afternoon, he'd asked her to marry him, and without one moment of hesitation, she'd said yes. They'd talked to the kids together and Adie had been delighted that Bray-Neigh was sticking around, and Keagan, well, he'd mumbled "Congratulations" and offered Bray a seat on the couch so he could watch some football.

He rubbed his thumb across Summer's palm. "I love you," he whispered.

"I've loved you forever," she whispered back, her pretty eyes shining.

And he knew that to be true.

* * * * *

Don't miss the conclusion of
Beverly Long's gripping miniseries
RETURN TO RAVESVILLE
when DEEP SECRETS goes on sale next month.
You'll find it wherever
Harlequin Intrigue books are sold!

LARGER-PRINT BOOKS!

HARLEQUIN

Presents®

GET 2 FREE LARGER-PRINT NOVELS PLUS 2 FREE GIFTS!

PASSION GUARANTEED SEDUCTION

YES! Please send me 2 FREE LARGER-PRINT Harlequin Presents® novels and my 2 FREE gifts (gifts are worth about $10). After receiving them, if I don't wish to receive any more books, I can return the shipping statement marked "cancel." If I don't cancel, I will receive 6 brand-new novels every month and be billed just $5.30 per book in the U.S. or $5.74 per book in Canada. That's a saving of at least 12% off the cover price! It's quite a bargain! Shipping and handling is just 50¢ per book in the U.S. and 75¢ per book in Canada.* I understand that accepting the 2 free books and gifts places me under no obligation to buy anything. I can always return a shipment and cancel at any time. Even if I never buy another book, the two free books and gifts are mine to keep forever.

176/376 HDN GHVY

Name _____ (PLEASE PRINT)

Address _____ Apt. #

City _____ State/Prov. _____ Zip/Postal Code

Signature (if under 18, a parent or guardian must sign)

Mail to the **Reader Service:**
IN U.S.A.: P.O. Box 1867, Buffalo, NY 14240-1867
IN CANADA: P.O. Box 609, Fort Erie, Ontario L2A 5X3

**Are you a subscriber to Harlequin Presents® books and want to receive the larger-print edition?
Call 1-800-873-8635 today or visit us at www.ReaderService.com.**

* Terms and prices subject to change without notice. Prices do not include applicable taxes. Sales tax applicable in N.Y. Canadian residents will be charged applicable taxes. Offer not valid in Quebec. This offer is limited to one order per household. Not valid for current subscribers to Harlequin Presents Larger-Print books. All orders subject to credit approval. Credit or debit balances in a customer's account(s) may be offset by any other outstanding balance owed by or to the customer. Please allow 4 to 6 weeks for delivery. Offer available while quantities last.

Your Privacy—The Reader Service is committed to protecting your privacy. Our Privacy Policy is available online at www.ReaderService.com or upon request from the Reader Service.

We make a portion of our mailing list available to reputable third parties that offer products we believe may interest you. If you prefer that we not exchange your name with third parties, or if you wish to clarify or modify your communication preferences, please visit us at www.ReaderService.com/consumerschoice or write to us at Reader Service Preference Service, P.O. Box 9062, Buffalo, NY 14240-9062. Include your complete name and address.

HPLP15

LARGER-PRINT BOOKS!
GET 2 FREE LARGER-PRINT NOVELS PLUS
2 FREE GIFTS!

HARLEQUIN®

Romance

From the Heart, For the Heart

LARGER-PRINT BOOKS!
GET 2 FREE LARGER-PRINT NOVELS PLUS
2 FREE GIFTS!

⊕ HARLEQUIN®

super romance®

More Story...More Romance

READERSERVICE.COM

Manage your account online!

- Review your order history
- Manage your payments
- Update your address

> *We've designed the*
> *Reader Service website*
> *just for you.*

Enjoy all the features!

- Discover new series available to you, and read excerpts from any series.
- Respond to mailings and special monthly offers.
- Connect with favorite authors at the blog.
- Browse the Bonus Bucks catalog and online-only exculsives.
- Share your feedback.

Visit us at:

ReaderService.com